MURDER IN THE COMMUNE

THE PRIVATE INVESTIGATOR ANNIE HUDSON
REAL ESTATE MYSTERY SERIES
BOOK 4

VALERIE BRANDY

Copyright © 2024 Valerie Brandy.

All rights reserved. No part of this book may be reproduced in any form or by any electronic or mechanical means, including information storage and retrieval systems, without permission in writing from the publisher, except by reviewers, who may quote brief passages in a review.

Published by: Emerald Lion Press.

23901 Calabasas Rd., Ste 2088,

Calabasas, CA 91302.

emeraldlionpress@gmail.com

This is a work of fiction. Names, characters, businesses, events, and incidents either are the products of the author's imagination or are used fictitiously. Any resemblance to actual persons, living or dead, businesses, companies, events, or locales is entirely coincidental.

ISBN: 978-1-964161-34-1

Editing provided by Sharon Lennon-Mehlschau.

To request permission to use passages from this book in any context other than a review, please contact the publisher at emeraldlionpress@gmail.com.

Visit the author's website at: www.valeriebrandy.com

❀ Created with Vellum

CONTENTS

CHAPTER ONE

IN THE TWO days since Private Investigator Annie Hudson and her partner— FBI Agent Ethan Beckett— had arrived at *Serenity Peaks*, the commune had lived up to its name. Snuggled up to the base of the Sierra Nevada Mountains, *Serenity Peaks* consisted of a cluster of identical log cabins surrounded by pine trees. Between them, a larger structure served as the kitchen and dining hall, and a community room allowed residents to host events. Out back, a series of private hot tubs permitted residents to lean back in the warm water, gazing past the peak of the enormous mountains into the starry night sky. The entire operation bordered the edge of a crystal-clear lake, trees reaching for the sky like sentinels protecting the commune from intruders. Intruders like Annie and Ethan.

The pair had ventured to the commune in hopes of interviewing a suspect, Russel Grey, who was unfortunately away on a trip when they'd arrived. Still, they'd enjoyed the vacation. All in all, *Serenity Peaks* was a nice place to disconnect from the real world.

At least, that's what Annie had been thinking when she

opened the door to the community room, only to find a dead body lying in the middle of the space.

"Russel?" A voice next to Annie called out. The voice belonged to Tania Wildheart, a plump, middle-aged woman who had introduced herself to Annie and Ethan as the de facto President of *Serenity Peaks*. The commune didn't believe in labels, but— as Tania had pointed out— someone had to run the place, and it might as well be her. She rushed across the room, pushing Annie and Ethan aside as she bent down next to the limp human form laying in the middle of the floor, leaning down to check if he was breathing.

The body belonged to Russel Grey— Annie's sole purpose for coming to the commune. He had arrived just hours ago, and Annie had set up a meeting in the community room in the hopes of interviewing him. Now, that seemed impossible. Foam coated his mouth, and his eyes were fixed toward the ceiling, seeing nothing there at all.

"He's—" Tania choked on her words, unable to say the terrible truth.

"Dead?" Annie answered, a calm tenor to her voice. "Figures," she added, shaking her head. Tania stared up at her in horror, her expression rattled.

"What my partner means to say," Ethan interjected, putting an arm on Annie's shoulder. "Is that we were here to speak to Russel about something important. And it's pretty telling that— on the day of our meeting— he turns up dead."

"Telling?" Tania blinked, her eyes wide. "What could you possibly mean? He was just out of town getting repair equipment for the generators and then he comes home and— and now—"

"He's dead," Annie nodded in agreement. "My point exactly. A perfectly healthy man leaves for a two-day trip. In that time, we arrive, hoping to speak with him. The same perfectly healthy man returns home and only a few hours after his arrival— and moments before our intended meeting — turns up dead. Suspicious, don't you think?"

Tania sat on her heels, brushing her hair out of her face. Dried flowers were woven into her braids, and a necklace of seashells dangled at her chest. "I don't think anything," Tania shook her head. "Except that it was an accident. It had to have been an accident. Things like this just don't happen at *Serenity Peaks*."

"They do now," Annie shrugged. Tania stared back at her with a blank expression. "You're in shock," Annie said. "Not to worry, we'll get to the bottom of this. Ethan?"

"I'll call it in," Ethan agreed.

Annie approached the body on the floor and leaned down to examine the man she had so badly wanted to meet. A grey mustache connected to a similar beard, and his face was wrinkled in the kind of way that made a person seem wise, and therefore trustworthy.

"What was it you wanted to talk to him about?" Tania asked, sensing for the first time that the two visitors she'd welcomed into the commune weren't actually old friends of Russel's after all.

"We have history," Annie said vaguely. "A mystery I was hoping Russel could help me solve. Although, I wasn't expecting him to help me in exactly this way." She motioned at the prostrate body in front of her.

Russel Grey was the answer to a mystery from Annie's past— the mystery of her brother's murder, as well as the disappearance of Ethan's sister. Annie's evidence had led her to this moment, and now— the main suspect was lying dead in front of her.

Still, victims could speak in their own quiet way, and Annie was of the opinion that Russel had a lot to say. She had hoped the lead would be straightforward, and now that Russel was her newest client, things had become considerably more complicated.

Annie turned back to Russel, scanning his face as if he were an old friend.

"Let's get to the bottom of it, shall we?" she asked him.

And with that, her investigation began.

CHAPTER TWO

TANIA

AFTER DISCOVERING Russel's body with the two visitors, Tania Wildheart spent the rest of the evening in a haze. The Police were called, and Tania watched as their squad cars pulled up in front of the small collection of cabins, red and blue lights coloring the night in a frightening, alien way. Tania hated seeing *Serenity Peaks* invaded by outsiders, all of them swarming like ants across the property, their crime tape and leather boots an unwelcome reminder that— outside of the commune— the world was a violent, terrible place. Still, despite her fears, Tania sucked in a deep breath and took on the difficult task of spearheading the operation, showing the Police the body and assuring them nobody at the commune would have had a reason to hurt Russel.

It had always been like this at *Serenity Peaks*. The commune didn't believe in hierarchical structures of leadership, and there was no official leader on the property. Still, Tania was the commune's longest-standing resident, and she had unofficially been put in charge when the property's founder died back in the seventies. Since then, she'd been doing everything in her power to make sure *Serenity Peaks* was the kind of idyllic retreat that showed the world what people were capable of at their best. Tania saw the commune as an example of how life *should* be lived. *Serenity Peaks* was proof that people could govern themselves, work as a team, and generally live peacefully all on their own accord.

Of course, this recent murder didn't do much to help that argument.

After touring the space with Annie and Ethan, the Police agreed to file an official report but leave the rest of the investigation up to the pair. Tania marveled at the impact the two partners seemed to have on the local law enforcement. She watched in amazement as Ethan flashed the head officer some kind of badge, after which the officer seemed to bend to Ethan's every will. Whoever these two people were, they seemed to be a very big deal in the world of law enforcement.

Tania stood outside with Annie and Ethan as Annie shook the head Officer's hand."We'll get that toxicology report back to you," the Officer said to Annie. "See if we can figure out what killed him."

Over his shoulder, Russel's body was wheeled out on a gurney, covered by a privacy tarp. Two first responders loaded him on the van, shutting the doors in the back with a thud.

"It was an accident of course," Tania said vaguely, aware that her own voice sounded very far away. "Nobody at *Serenity Peaks* would want to hurt Russel."

The Detectives surrounding her exchanged sideways glances. "Ma'am," the Officer said gently. "I hate to tell you this, but judging by the foam around his mouth and the fact he was previously in excellent health, this has all the markings of a poisoning."

Poison? The idea seemed laughable. But then, Tania was struck by a realization. Something she hadn't put together until just now. The flash of understanding must have shown on her face as horror, because the Officer reached out and touched her arm.

"Don't worry," he nodded. "Lucky for you, you've got two of the best Detectives in the world on your case." He glanced at Annie and Ethan, admiration lighting up his eyes. "These two are bloodhounds. Annie here has quite the reputation. She can get to the bottom of anything. You'll find out what happened to Russel in no time. The guilty party won't even know what hit 'em."

The guilty party. Tania's ears rang, her head suddenly lighter. "Well," she smiled at the Officer. "That certainly is reassuring."

The hours that followed were a painful blur. Tania allowed the Police to search the area for fingerprints and evidence, with Annie and Ethan leading the charge. In the middle of it all, Tania comforted multiple grieving residents and welcomed a new one who had chosen the most terrible of all evenings to join the commune. Through it all, her mind was elsewhere, distracted by something that lurked in her cabin.

Later— when the Police had left, and the flashing lights were gone— Tania escorted Annie and Ethan back to the cabin they'd been sharing. Then, she returned to her private lodgings, which were nestled on the edge of the co-op, furthest from the rest of the collective. The cabin's heavy, wooden door squeaked as she opened it without the need to unlock it— here, everyone trusted each other.

Tania closed the door behind her, looking around her space. It was a quaint, studio cottage consisting of one room. In the corner sat a small table with a collection of chairs surrounding it. A twin-sized bed was pushed against the opposite wall. The room was small, but it was all Tania needed.

With a sense of urgency, Tania ran to a narrow wardrobe that served as the room's only closet. She pushed the sliding doors open, sinking to her knees and feeling toward the back of the space until her fingers connected with a small, wooden box. She pulled it out and opened it up, revealing dried flowers within.

The flowers were purple and grew upright in the valleys surrounding the commune, their stalks reaching for the sky in friendly clusters. They were easy enough to find for anyone willing to take a short walk through the forest. Scientists knew them as the genus *Lupinus Grayi* flower, but common gardeners called them Gray's Lupine. They were charming and added a beautiful spray of color to any garden.

They also happened to be incredibly poisonous. *Especially* when consumed in large quantities.

And— just last night— a member of the commune had asked Tania for a cluster of the plants. At the time, Tania had thought nothing of it. The Lupine— when soaked in a tea— could be used to treat insomnia in small amounts. She'd assumed the individual who asked her to share the plants was merely hoping to address a bout of insomnia.

But now, with Russel dead and the foam around his mouth a clear indication of poisoning, Tania wondered if she had made a huge mistake.

She took the brown box to the toilet and flipped it upside down, letting the rest of the dried flowers spill onto the top of the water, where they floated in place. She pulled a drop-down silver cord from the ceiling and the toilet roared to life with a flushing sound, the water swirling in a spiral until every last petal disappeared.

Then, she peeked out her window to make sure no one was standing outside and opened the front door, marching to a set of planter boxes on her cabin's wrap-around porch. She reached into the planter box, pulling up a set of purple flowers by their roots. More Lupine. She made sure the planter box was empty, then carried the plants back into the bathroom and flushed them down the toilet as well for good measure.

When the job was done, Tania noticed the empty box sitting on the bathroom sink. She returned the box to its place in her closet and climbed into bed, turning on her side and wondering at the way life could change in an instant.

CHAPTER THREE

FLEUR

FLEUR MEADOWS HAD WATCHED the Police arrive from the top of a hiking trail that wove its way behind the plot of land that belonged to *Serenity Peaks*. She was a wisp of a woman in her twenties who had displayed a persistent childlike energy. Maybe it was her small frame or the angles of her jaw, but there was an innocence to Fleur that made people think she was much younger than her actual age. Little did they know how much life had taught her.

Fleur crouched on a fallen log behind a cluster of trees, peering through the branches to gape at the cadets, who descended upon the commune like flies on meat. She clutched a sketchbook in her hands, an artist's bag of tools beside it. Crouched on the ground, she flipped to a new page and— with a set of watercolor pencils— began to draw the scene unfolding down the hill. A quick sketch of a police car. A color rendition of the ambulance, a pale shade of red mimicking the real thing. Fleur's hands worked quickly and nimbly, the act of creating art transforming her pain, as it always did. The entire process took more than an hour. Finally, Fleur noticed a gurney with a figure on top being loaded into a white van and stopped drawing. This was one moment she didn't want to record. She knew the worst was over.

Russel's body had been removed.

Fleur never saw his face during the rush of activity, but she knew by the gurney he was dead. Tears streaked down her cheeks. She crouched motionless on the log, watching as the cadets tore down their crime tape. The moment was over.

For the first time in her life, Fleur was confronted with a feeling too big for her pencils and sketchbook to fix.

She shivered, thinking about what she had left to do. Her mind flashed back to a conversation she'd had with Russel many weeks ago. He'd asked her to do something. And now, she was left to carry out his work alone.

She clutched her sketchbook close to her chest. Her love of art had supported her through the worst moments of her life. She would need that creative strength to carry out the rest of the plan.

Fleur pulled her knees up to her chest, not bothering to wipe away the fresh tears that spilled down her cheeks in an angry, emotional flurry.

There was still more to do.

CHAPTER FOUR

MARK

MARK WAYANS WAS PERFORMING maintenance on *Serenity Peaks'* only vehicle when he heard Tania's scream coming from the community room. He had been situated underneath the pick-up truck on his back, his weight evenly dispersed across a rolling dolly when the sound caught his attention. It was strange, now, to think that— while Mark was underneath the truck— Russel was also lying on his back, albeit for a very different reason.

Although Mark heard the commotion, he chose not to go to the community room and investigate. Instead, he slid out from underneath the truck and wiped his hands on a rag, opening the hood and investigating the oil converter within. This truck was special. It ran only on corn oil and had a net zero impact on the environment. It was, in Mark's view, more environmentally friendly than electric, and could be the answer to climate change if enough people were willing to sacrifice for the greater good.

Mark wiped his hands on the towel, thinking about the vehicle and the sacrifices people were willing to make for each other. Mark was in his late fifties, grey-haired, and smart enough to know you had to help people when you could without expecting much from it. Mark had given the truck to Russel, who had just returned from a trip into town for supplies. The two men shared ownership of the vehicle, but— predictably— it had fallen on Mark to perform the necessary maintenance, as it always did.

This wasn't the first time Mark had decided to help Russel Grey and found himself worse off for it.

In fact, he had once helped Russel with an activity that involved two people he had seen just moments earlier, accompanying Tania into the community room. The pair he had come to know as Annie and Ethan. Although he hadn't met them in person until two days ago, Mark was familiar with who they were. Their arrival had taken him by surprise, but when he connected it with Russel's absence, the picture started to make sense.

Leave it to Russel to expect the rest of us to sort out the problem, Mark had thought to himself.

As an environmentalist, Mark was particularly sensitive to the idea that many problems required the power of the collective to be solved. He'd spent decades working for a climate change think-tank on the East Coast, only to retire early when he realized absolutely nothing he was doing was making any difference whatsoever. When he came to *Serenity Peaks,* he found a fresh start. This was a place where nobody spoke about the past. In fact, the number one rule in the Commune was simply:

Do not ask another member about their life before they arrived.

The second rule was just as easy to follow:

Do not talk about your own life before you arrived.

And that's what made Mark's current predicament so frustrating in Mark's eyes. He had come to this place to start over, but Russel had insisted on breaking the first two rules, sucking Mark into his past. Now, Mark knew something he shouldn't know. And he was responsible for more than he wanted to be responsible for. Mark had come to the commune in hopes of finding people who put others before themselves, and— in his eyes— Russel had been a bit selfish, dragging him into a mess. He was angry at Russel, and cleaning out the truck after another one of Russel's selfish expeditions only ignited his fury. As he ran clean water through the corn oil engine, he considered how Russel hadn't even bothered to say "thank you." When Russel arrived just five hours earlier, he'd simply dropped the keys to the truck into Mark's hands, then rushed off without saying much at all. He'd briefly mentioned the "engine seemed flooded," and left a mountain of crumpled fast-food bags in the backseat. Typical Russel.

Mark continued calmly working on the truck throughout the evening, even nodding at the Police Officers as they arrived. The presence of the Officers concerned Mark, but he thought perhaps Tania's scream could have been related to wildlife, like a stray bear. Maybe they'd come to assist animal services. Whatever the problem was, Mark resisted the urge to go check on the community room. He'd done enough self-less tasks as of late, and where had it gotten him? Elbow deep in a flooded engine, that's where.

One cadet had approached him, notebook in hand, a pleasant-enough look on his face.

"Excuse me, sir," the young Officer nodded at him. He looked new to the force, not older than twenty-five. "Not sure how long you've been working on the truck, but did you happen to see anything suspicious tonight?"

Mark leaned against the truck, setting the wrench he was holding onto the hood with a clatter. "Been out here a few hours," Mark said carefully. "Didn't see anything strange. Just heard a commotion and then you all showed up." He paused, looking the Officer up and down. "Is everything okay in there? What is it? A bear?"

"Afraid not," the Cadet sighed. "A man's been murdered."

Mark's heart tightened in his chest. *Murdered?* Things like that didn't happen here.

"Who?" Mark asked, fearing that perhaps he already knew the answer.

The Officer glanced at his notebook. "Russel Grey?" He said Russel's name as if it were a question. Mark shivered as his fear was confirmed.

Russel, he thought. *Why couldn't you leave the past alone?* "No," Mark said, shaking his head. "That— can't be—" Mark leaned against the truck, the tightness in his chest growing so firm he thought he might be having a heart attack. He put a hand to his chest, trying to catch his breath. Suddenly, his anger at Russel seemed stupid. Mark rifled through his memories, trying to recall the last words he'd said to the man.

Mark's emotion wasn't lost on the Cadet, who put a hand on his shoulder. "I'm sorry for your loss," the Officer answered, appearing to genuinely mean it. "Were you close with him?"

The question jolted Mark back into the moment, and he was struck by the urge to defend himself. "Officer," Mark said, throwing his hands in the air. "Look around. This is a commune. Of course we were close."

The Officer blushed. He put his notebook away, sensing he'd done all he could, here. "Thank you for your time," he said, shuffling away. "Sorry, again."

Mark turned his back on the officer, swallowing the shame he felt rising up in his throat. He had downplayed his connection to Russel. Betrayed him. Mark shook the feeling off, returning his attention to the well of the truck, but thinking all the while about the mess Russel had made. And now, he'd summoned two detectives to the commune:

Two detectives who just might ruin everything.

And just like those fast-food bags in the backseat, Russel had hoped Mark would clean it up.

Nope, Mark thought, shaking his head, anger churning

deep within him. *Not this time, Russel.* And in that moment, Mark did something he'd never done before.

He planned to break a promise to someone he cared about.

CHAPTER FIVE

GURU METT

WHEN GURU METT saw the Police cars arrive, he knew something awful had happened.

Guru Mett had been standing outside his private bungalow when the red and blue lights spilled across the street that led to the commune, leaning over his tomato plants with a set of sheers. Guru Mett was a plump man in his late seventies who loved to garden, and he'd managed to grow an impressive crop. Vegetables bordered the Western side of his prized showcase. Tomatoes. Cucumbers. Peppers. A bounty of color peaked out from the soil, tiny signs designating each specific plant. On the opposite side, flowers grew in clusters of cotton-candy petals. Violets. Petunias. Vining plants laced up trellises. Guru Mett enjoyed gardening because it reminded him that a person didn't need money to provide for themselves in life.

That's what had brought Guru Mett to *Serenity Peaks* in the first place— the pursuit of a life outside of money. Money had defined him before he'd begun again in *Serenity Peaks*. Since his arrival, he'd taken on the informal label of "Guru," and had committed to help both himself and other members of the Commune find their connection to the divine. In the back of his bungalow was a private meditation center, complete with contemplative floor- pillows, fountains, chimes, and incense always at the ready. In that sacred space, Guru Mett had met with many members of the commune, always ready to hear their troubles. *Serenity Peaks'* members had cried in his presence, laughed with him, and shared their deepest concerns, always leaving with a newfound sense of peace thanks to his guidance.

He gave them comfort while allowing them to let go of the past. Because, in *Serenity Peaks*, the number one rule was that members didn't talk about their pasts.

But— in front of Guru Mett— many of the members of the commune had broken this promise. They'd trusted him with the deepest parts of themselves, and he had done his best to honor their wishes by keeping the secrets of their pasts close to the vest. They'd revealed themselves fully, flaws and all— an act Guru Mett had not yet been able to bring himself to do within his own life.

He thought about this fact later as he watched, trance-like, while a pair of first responders wheeled Russel's cloaked body into a white van.

Unable to bear the sight of it all anymore, Guru Mett put down his trimming sheers and retreated into his bungalow, heading toward the private meditation room at the back of his lodgings. He opened the door, inhaling the sweet scent of cedar wood. Overhead, a warm light fixture glistened. Plump pillows decorated the space. A pair of glass sliding doors on the opposite wall opened out to a natural clearing at the base of the mountain. Sometimes, deer or other wildlife would venture there, blessing Guru Mett with the pleasure of their company.

Guru Mett glanced out the sliding doors to ensure no one was watching— deer *or* human— then, he made his way to a floorboard in the corner of the room. He pressed hard on the edge of the plank, and it rose up with ease, revealing hidden space underneath. Guru Mett reached into the hole, removing a laptop computer.

Such devices were banned at *Serenity Peaks*, but Guru Mett was a person who had always struggled to avoid his vices. There was a weak WIFI signal on the mountain from a satellite dish, but it was supposed to be used only in emergencies.

He held the laptop in his hands, thinking about what Russel had asked him to do. He had promised he would conduct this final act for his friend. But now that the moment had arrived, it seemed too big a task.

Telling them could destroy me, Guru Mett thought to himself, a shiver running down his spine. Now that *Serenity Peaks* was crawling with law enforcement, Russel's request seemed too great.

Guru Mett considered, then slid the laptop back into its hidden compartment.

He would wait, he decided, for the proper moment. He would allow the scene to unfold, determine who he could trust, and then— and only then— he would make any moves.

CHAPTER SIX

CORD

CORD SMITH WAS *SERENITY PEAKS*' youngest resident. At nineteen, he'd lived his whole life suspecting that something was seriously, terribly wrong with him. And when he saw the EMTs removing Russel's body from the community center, he knew, without a shadow of a doubt— that he was right.

"Where are you taking him?" Cord cried out, trying to stop the men pushing the gurney from moving any further. He didn't know when he'd started crying, but hot, wet tears, slipped down his face anyway. Suddenly, a pair of arms wrapped around his waist. It was Tania Wildheart, the commune's de facto leader, looking just as upset on the outside as Cord felt on the inside.

"You have to let him go," Tania whispered in his ear. "Come here, sweetheart. It's going to be okay."

Even though he could have overpowered Tania with ease, Cord allowed her to usher him away from the scene, one arm over his shoulder. Cord hiccupped, a deep anger welling up inside of him.

"They're just taking him away and they haven't even looked into anything!" Cord practically shouted at Tania, wiping snot from his nose. "Russel *said* this would happen. He told me—"

"They are looking into it," Tania assured Cord. "There's two detectives here. They're the best in the world. They'll figure out what happened."

"They need to get the people who did this! Russel told me that he might not always be around and if anything ever happened to him I should—"

"Shhh," Tania shook her head, a scolding look in her eye. "What do we leave behind?"

Cord exhaled, trying to get his breathing to return to a normal rate. "The past," he said, repeating *Serenity Peaks'* number one rule.

Tania nodded. "If Russel told you something about his past, that was a mistake. But you must put it out of your mind. The Detectives are going to take care of this. Just give them time. There will be justice for Russel, you have my word," she said, reassuring herself as much as Cord. "These Detectives are going to look into everyone and everything. All secrets will be revealed. Nobody can hide from them."

Nobody can hide, Cord thought to himself, an icy horror suddenly running through his veins. He'd just realized something. Something terrible. Something he hadn't considered until now.

Zombie-like, Cord allowed Tania to offer a few more comforting platitudes, then made his way back to his quaint bungalow that was positioned at the foot of the mountain. Cord stumbled back to his home in the dark, the hooting of an owl overhead his only company. He had walked through the commune many times in the dark of the night, but this evening, the black blanket of nightfall felt too heavy to bear. Then, he saw the warmth of the lantern he kept on his front porch beaming back at him, lit at all times so he could find his way home.

Cord stumbled up the steps, accidentally knocking over a

metal bucket with a broom inside. As the Commune's de facto groundskeeper, Cord was responsible for keeping the group facilities clean. He performed maintenance on the hot tub. Kept the dining hall sparkling. And— just this morning— had cleaned the community room from top to bottom. He hated to think that Russel had met his end in a space he'd been attending to just hours earlier.

Cord opened the door to his bungalow, barely noticing his unkempt bed or messy fireplace. Cord may have kept the commune clean for others, but rarely worried about the state of his own space. He made his way to the bathroom, pushing open the door with a guilty look on his face. There, on the sink, was arranged a little shrine of sorts.

There sat a woman's headband, made from lace and viscose. A man's wallet, emptied out of all cards or cash. A golden hoop earring, abandoned and separated from its mate. And most importantly, a plastic entry card with a familiar name on the front: RUSSEL GREY.

Cord grabbed the card off the edge of the sink, new tears forming in his eyes. Then, he layed down in his small, twin-sized bed, clutching the card to his heart.

Russel had been his friend. And now, he was gone. Cord worried that the two detectives would find out his secret, and take away the rest of his friends, too. He glanced at the sink, where the objects stood in a line. They reminded him of soldiers in a firing squad, all of them pointing… at *him*.

CHAPTER SEVEN

BANKS

BANKS HAD CHOSEN an unfortunate time to arrive at his new home in *Serenity Peaks.*

He had just pulled up to the Commune via a very expensive car ride from town when Russel Grey turned up dead. As Banks' car dropped him off at the top of the narrow, dirt road that led to *Serenity Peaks*, Banks was surprised to see a collection of Police Cars gathered in the driveway, their headlights a symphony of eyes staring straight at him.

Banks pushed his duffel bag higher on his shoulder, all of his worldly possessions contained within. He strode toward the cabins, stopping to ask an Officer what had happened.

"A man was poisoned," the Officer answered, writing something down on his notepad. "You're new here?" He asked.

"Newest member," Banks said brightly, pushing his glasses higher up on his nose. Banks prided himself on his intellectual appearance. He wore black- rimmed glasses, a flannel shirt, and kept this facial hair in an immaculately- groomed pattern, completing the look with a man-bun pulled tight on the back of his head. He looked like many urban hipsters in cities across the world— the difference being that Banks was a man who was willing to live his convictions and not just "talk" about them. That's why he had moved to *Serenity Peaks*. Banks was a man of action.

"You might want to talk to her," the Officer pointed at a woman with flowers in her hair. Banks recognized her immediately as Tania Wildheart, who he'd spoken to over Zoom before signing up to join the commune. Tania had answered his questions and made him feel right at home.

Banks waved at Tania, who ran toward him. "My goodness," she said, slapping her forehead. "I completely forgot about your arrival— in all the uproar—"

"What's happened?" Banks said, his eyes narrowing. "The Officer said someone was murdered?"

"You have to understand, this kind of thing just doesn't happen here. We've never had anything like this occur on the property. *Serenity Peaks* is a safe place..."

Banks' stomach flipped over, a nauseous feeling making his throat tighten. "Who was killed?" He said, fearing that he'd made a terrible mistake accepting this challenge.

"Russel Grey," Tania offered, a sad tone coloring her voice a hundred shades of blue. "He was a wonderful man. I'm so sad you'll never meet him."

Banks' jaw set in a steely hard line as he shifted his duffel bag to his other shoulder. It suddenly felt very heavy. "So am I," Banks said, really meaning it.

This new development complicated everything, and suddenly Banks resented the long ride in the car up a winding mountain road. Because the truth was— Banks had *very* much been looking forward to meeting Mr. Russel Grey.

"I'll show you to your cabin, then?" Tania said, grabbing Banks by the elbow and leading him toward a bungalow in the middle of the group. Banks allowed her to escort him to his new home, trying all the while to hide his upset. After unlocking the door to his cabin and passing him the key, Tania showed him how to work a landline phone that was plugged into the corner. She opened the linen cabinet to offer him fresh bedding. Once the initial tour was done, Tania reminded Banks of the commune's main rules.

"No talking about your past or asking other members about their own histories," Tania said. "*Serenity Peaks* is a place for fresh starts. We like everyone to begin anew."

"I remember from our Zoom call," Banks agreed.

"That's another important thing," Tania continued. "No cell phones, computers, or internet. We *do* allow residents to use the computer in the community room for three-hour time slots each Friday, but otherwise, we live *presently*." She held out her arms by her side and took a deep inhale, closing her eyes as if she were standing on the edge of a mountaintop. "We live for the *moment*, not as ideas inside a machine. The lack of technology allows us all to connect with each other. Landline phones are permitted," she nodded at the rotary phone on his nightstand. "But we really encourage residents to be part of the community and give themselves the gift of connecting with others."

"Sounds great," Banks answered.

"And the name you'd like to go by? Is it still the same one you used to register?"

That's right. Banks had forgotten. Every resident was allowed to use a new name upon signing up for the commune. It was part of their "leave the past behind" nonsense.

"Banks is great," he said, shrugging. He hadn't used his birth name in a long time anyway. He'd signed up under Banks because it was one of his favorite aliases. Why change now?

"Excellent," Tania said, patting his hand. "I'll introduce you to the group that way. Tomorrow, of course. It's going to be a difficult day, but we'll get through it together."

You have no idea, Banks thought to himself. He waited until Tania had left, shutting the cabin's wooden door behind her.

He lifted back the curtain in the window, watching as she strode across the grounds and out of sight.

Then, he reached into his duffel bag and ripped away a patch of fabric, revealing something hidden in the lining: a cell phone. He opened up his text messages and sent a few words to a familiar number:

BANKS

We have a problem.

CHAPTER EIGHT

FOR ANNIE AND ETHAN, the night was long. From the moment they discovered the body of Russel Grey, time seemed to warp into one twisting, undefinable spiral. The Police Chief— who oversaw not just *Serenity Peaks* but multiple towns down the mountain resting at lower altitudes — was more than happy to turn over responsibility for the case to the pair as outside specialists given Annie's reputation and Ethan's FBI affiliation. The subsequent hours were spent creating a plan for moving forward, from the sharing of information to toxicology reports. Annie and Ethan evaluated the community room alongside Officers, searching the space for signs of a struggle, of which there were none. When the last police cruiser pulled out of the driveway, it was three in the morning, and Annie felt her legs ready to collapse underneath her.

Ethan seemed to notice and linked his arm around Annie's. "Time to call it a night," he told her. They were alone outside the community building, and the sudden silence was jarring. The woman who oversaw the commune— Tania Wildheart— had long since retired to her cabin, and the few members of the commune who had peaked out in curiosity had likewise retreated into their cabins. Without the scuffle of Police boots on the dirt, the forest was silent once again. Stars twinkled overhead, and the soft chirping of crickets did little to fill the space.

"To bed," Annie agreed, thinking about how much she hated silence. It was in the quiet moments that Annie was able to think about what bothered her most in the world. Her aversion to silence was one of the things she loved most about solving mysteries. Putting together a puzzle gave her something to occupy her busy mind, which would go in the wrong direction if left without an activity.

Leaves crunched under Annie's feet as the pair made their way back to the small Bungalow they'd begun to call home. They'd only arrived at the commune two days ago, but the cabin had a vintage energy that made it easy for a person to relax into the space. Mustard yellow curtains dangled from the ceiling, and a paisley wallpaper decorated the back wall. It was a one room studio, but featured its own little kitchen and a tidy, quaint bathroom with crystal pull- knobs on the vanity. A soft, clean rug decorated the floor, and the entire effect made Annie think it might have been the best place they'd ever stayed in.

Ethan hopped into the shower as Annie collapsed onto the bed, lamenting the lack of a television. That was one thing she hadn't gotten used to in *Serenity Peaks*— the absence of technology. Still, there was always books. Annie considered pulling out one of the paperbacks that were stacked on the bookshelf that came with the cabin, but she was too tired to move from the bed. Instead, she listened to the water run, knowing that it was ice cold. Ethan took his showers short and painful, never so much as turning the water hot.

The water shut off, and Ethan emerged from the bathroom, a towel wrapped around his waist. He shut the door behind him and flicked off the lights, leaving nothing but the bedside lamp on. He climbed into bed next to Annie and wrapped his arms around her, kissing her ear.

"We're closer," he said, keeping his voice down even though no one else was around. "We can solve the past."

"I don't know if anyone can solve the past," Annie said her voice hollow.

"Hey," Ethan rested his head on his arm, sitting up to get a better look at her. "You might be right about that. But we move toward a better future."

"I just can't believe— we get here and our main suspect is dead."

"Doesn't matter," Ethan shrugged. "Annie, I've never met anyone with a mind like yours. You can do anything. This is a huge lead, and it's one you'll unwind, even if the main suspect is dead."

Annie stared into his eyes, so hopeful and assured. His confidence in her made her want to look away. "I know it's naive, but I just hoped—"

"What?"

"I hoped it would be easy," Annie shrugged. "I hoped we'd get here and Russel Grey would throw up his hands and say 'Alright, you caught me. I'm the notorious serial killer you've been looking for who killed people you loved.'"

"Wow," Ethan nodded. "That's surprisingly optimistic, coming from you."

"And now he can't tell us what happened because he's dead," she said, looking up at the ceiling and trying to count the dots there. "I'm tired of solving other people's mysteries but never being able to crack my own."

Her cheeks flushed as she admitted the truth aloud. Annie loved the satisfaction she got from helping others find resolution in the face of a violent crime. But with each victim brought to justice— with each family member given closure— Annie couldn't help but feel the little wound within her chest deepen.

"It's like I'm cursed," she said. "I can only solve the mysteries that won't bring me any closer to feeling…"

"Whole," Ethan nodded, understanding. He took her hands in his.

"Maybe we should walk away," Annie said, looking out the window. She thought about what the world had taught her about life so far: that one must be able to take care of herself. The world was a cold place of brutal competition. Annie had spent most of her days in run-down motels and on big city streets, seeing the worst that the world had to offer. Since the death of her brother, the only person Annie had truly ever trusted was Ethan— and even *that* had taken more than a decade and a shared past. "This place— these people— they deserve better than me right now."

"I know it feels like we're farther away now that Russel is dead, but I think we might be closer than you realize."

"Why?" Annie asked.

"Whoever took him out didn't want him talking. It's confirmation we're on the right trail. This is big, Annie. Whatever's going on here feels like it's more than a lone operative."

Annie thought about Ethan's words as if emerging from a haze. She sat up as if she'd been hit by lightning, shocked she'd never considered such a thing. "It *does* seem bigger, doesn't it? The fact they had such technological capabilities. Even Milo struggled to get through the proxies. And they knew how to get a message to me. And now Russel—"

"Exactly," Ethan nodded. "In the FBI we look for known associates and grade the strength of the connection. We're trained to look for indicators of a cell organization. This has all the elements…"

Annie's mouth dropped open, sadness flashing in her eyes. "You saw it and I didn't." She paused, considering her own blind spots. "I've been so alone in the world, I assumed whoever did this must feel the same. But you're right— it can't be one person—"

"Nature likes to build systems," Ethan agreed. "Evil finds its match."

"And what about good?" Annie said, rolling over. "Does good ever find its match?" .

"People weren't meant to be alone, Annie," Ethan said.

He kissed her, and the sound of crickets chirping colored the night. Annie leaned against his chest as she closed her eyes, thinking about Russel Grey, and wondering what secrets he'd possessed worth dying for. She tried to believe what Ethan said. She tried to believe that people weren't meant to be alone. But she couldn't help but think that— in a world so brutal— being alone seemed like the smartest way to survive. Was it possible Russel had reached a different conclusion, and had paid the price with his life?

CHAPTER NINE

THE NEXT MORNING, Ethan awoke to find himself alone in the bed, a vacant imprint beside him where Annie had been sleeping. He sat up, rubbing his eyes and scanning the small bungalow for any sign of the woman he loved: she wasn't there. Then, he noticed the curtain had been pulled back, revealing a view out the window of the small porch that circled their cabin. Annie was sitting in the rocking chair with a cup of coffee in her hands.

Ethan stood, throwing on a pair of sweatpants and a t-shirt, then exited the front door. The crisp, morning air opened up his lungs as he sat next to Annie.

"Well?" Ethan asked. He knew she'd spent the night thinking, in and out of slumber, as she so often did. He could only guess at what conclusion she'd reached about life, and the mystery of Russel's death, and the long road that was opening in front of them.

She turned, and he was relieved to see she was smiling, her eyes alight once again with the fire that pushed her forward even in the most impossible of circumstances.

"Well, what?" Annie clucked, a teasing tone to her voice.

"It's a beautiful morning, and—" She paused, looking out at the vast forest in front of them.

"And?"

"And we have a job to do."

———

Later, Annie and Ethan met the rest of the commune in the dining building for breakfast. The dining building was a large, log cabin featuring a circular table at which all members could be seated in an egalitarian fashion. Behind the table, a stone fireplace blazed, and two bookshelves adorned the wall. A pair of couches were situated in front of the fire, for game nights and conversations into the evening. At the back of the cabin, an open-concept kitchen displayed a state-of-the-art Viking oven, and wide, commercial-grade cabinets framing a stainless-steel refrigerator. The commune was a forty-minute drive from the nearest supply store, and ensuring space for food supplies was— as Annie had learned— a priority for the group. Tania had explained that they took turns overseeing the preparation of various meals and made a once-a-week trip into town to garner the necessary supplies. This morning, it was Tania's turn to cook breakfast, and she had provided the group with a beautiful spread of freshly baked muffins, breadsticks, scrambled eggs, and bacon, all of it spread across the kitchen countertops in silver catering containers.

Now, the group was seated at the table, each of them having made their own plate. Glasses of orange juice clinked, but nobody spoke. Instead, all eyes were on Tania, waiting. She cleared her throat, flames in the fireplace crackling behind her.

"As many of you know, Russel Grey was pronounced dead last night," Tania said, looking down at the table.

Annie scanned the room to gauge the reactions of the residents. Next to Tania, the young woman— Fleur Meadows— dabbed at her eyes with a napkin, looking genuinely distressed. Beside her, Guru Mett shifted in his seat, plucking at his beard before patting her shoulder thoughtfully. On the opposite end of the table, Mark sat stone-faced, his jaw set in a tight, angry square that made his mandible muscle twitch. Next to him was Cord Smith, who Annie had come to know as the groundskeeper. He was young— barely out of his teens — and seemed to Annie to be somewhere on the spectrum. Judging by the tears streaming down his cheeks, he wasn't a person who could hide his emotions with ease. Finally, next to Ethan sat a new member of the commune who Annie had not yet met, but who had arrived last night.

"It's painful to lose one of our own," Tania said, placing her hands on the table like she was a President addressing the American people from the Oval Office. "But we must soldier on. The Police believe he was poisoned—"

Mark gasped then recovered, taking a sip of his orange juice with an unsteady hand. "Poisoned?" He said, choking back emotion.

"That's what they believe at this time," Tania nodded. "Thankfully, two of our most recent arrivals are also world-class detectives who have agreed to take on the case."

All heads swiveled toward Annie and Ethan, who sat in place as if they dared not move a muscle.

"Doesn't that seem weird?" Cord asked, choking on his croissant a little. "I mean, you two show up and then Russel dies and you just *happen* to be detectives."

Annie noted the flush in Cord's face. His cheeks were red, the emotion of anger readable in his eyes. Annie cleared her throat and stood, sensing what she needed to do.

"Cord," she smiled at him. "You are— absolutely right."

Murmurs echoed around the table at this astounding confession.

"It is very strange," Annie continued. "That Ethan and I

arrived just two days before Russel's murder. And, in the interest of friendship and the spirit of this commune, which thrives on— what was it?"

"Connection," Tania nodded.

"*Connection*," Annie smiled. "In the interest of that, I'm going to be honest with you. Ethan and I arrived at this commune with one intention only— to speak to Russel Grey. And I'm very concerned that our arrival may have been the triggering factor that led to his death."

More murmurs drifted across the table as Guru Mett whispered something to Fleur, who didn't react, but instead sat frozen, sculpture-like in her chair.

"I believe someone here wanted Russel Grey dead because of what he would have told us. And I'm going to find out who poisoned him. With your help, of course." She smiled cheerfully, as if she had just asked them all to a dance.

"How could we help?" Guru Mett asked, leaning forward over his eggs. He wore a beanie cap on his head and reached back to adjust it slightly. "None of us know what happened to Russel."

"One of you *certainly* knows what happened to Russel Grey," Annie said. "But that's neither here nor there. It's not the information I receive from any one person that matters most, but the picture as a whole. Each and every one of you could have something valuable to contribute. I hope you'll be honest with me. No matter how small you think a detail may be, I need the truth about it. Can we agree?" Annie asked, motioning around the table.

Six pairs of eyes blinked back at her. No one offered affirmation. Tania cleared her throat, breaking the silence.

"Annie will be conducting individual interviews throughout the week. I assured her we would all cooperate, given the spirit of community in our small cooperative."

Agreement sprung from around the table.

"Of course we will. It's spiritually correct," Guru Mett offered.

"Anything for Russel—" Cord said, his voice strained and tight with emotion.

"—willing to help in way possible—" Mark muttered.

"Only just got here, but I'll add what I can," Banks nodded.

"Why should we trust you?" Fleur's clear voice broke through the crowd. She stared at Annie. There was a stinging moment of discomfort as the rest of the table stared at her. Fleur looked at the other members of the commune in earnest, her cheeks flushed, eyes watering. "What?" She turned back to Annie. "You just arrived here, and now Russel's dead. How do we *know* it's safe to talk to you? What if we tell you something and we end up just like he did?"

Annie nodded gravely, as if she agreed that Fleur was making a very serious point. "You're absolutely right," Annie said. "I have to agree that— until we figure out what happened to Russel—no one here is safe. As no one else was on the property at the time, the killer was almost certainly a resident of the commune. In other words, the killer is likely sitting at this very table."

Sideways glances crossed the circular dining table. Guru Mett subtly slid his orange juice away from Fleur, as if he'd only just remembered that Russel was poisoned, and he didn't trust her near his glass. The movement wasn't lost on Fleur, who gave him a skeptical glare.

"Really?"

"I was just thirsty," Guru Mett said defensively, taking a small sip of his juice, but looking fearful as he swallowed.

"The point is," Annie continued. "You have every right to be concerned about your safety. But I believe you all came to this commune seeking the elevation of the greater good of the whole above the selfish interests of the individual. I'm asking you to help me because Russel was your friend. And he deserves justice."

A few nods around the table told Annie she'd made her point.

"I couldn't have said it better!" Tania Wildheart agreed, clapping her hands together. "Which brings me to our next order of breakfast business. We have a new guest. Everyone, please welcome Banks in the *Serenity Peaks* way."

Sighing, the group stood, forming a line in front of Banks, who looked rather alarmed at this new development. "Oh, they don't have to—" He started to say before Tania interrupted him.

"Nonsense, it's *Serenity Peaks* tradition."

Guru Mett was first in line. He took both his hands and put one of each on Banks' shoulder. Then, he leaned his forehead onto Banks' forehead and said, "I'm here for you."

"Um, thanks?" Banks said, clearly uncomfortable with the overture.

Next, Fleur stepped up, performing the same movements of two hands on each shoulder and the pressing of her forehead to his. One by one, each member of the commune assured Banks of their support, stating, "I'm here for you."

When everyone had completed the task, Tania couldn't help but look at Annie and Ethan, a hopeful glint in her eye. "Would you care to..."

Ethan cut off the possibility before Tania could even offer it as an idea. "Oh, we're good." Ethan said. "Professional line and all."

"You'll fall in love with us yet!" Tania laughed at him. "The welcome is a reminder that in *Serenity Peaks*, we're all here for each other."

"Well, we *were*," Guru Mett said absent-mindedly, stirring his orange juice around with a breadstick, looking into the glass as if it might hold answers to a bothersome question. When he looked up, he was surprised to find the rest of the group staring at him. "Oh, I just meant—" he stuttered.

"Russel is— dead. So— not so much with the 'here for you' thing. At least, not for him."

And with that, Tania clapped her hands, ready to end the breakfast.

"Banks, I'll take you on the welcome tour!" She turned to Annie and Ethan. "Would you two care to join us?"

"Actually," Annie nodded, squeezing Ethan's elbow before he could decline. "That seems like a great idea."

CHAPTER TEN

BANKS

BANKS FOLLOWED Tania through the commune, very aware of Annie and Ethan on his flank. They followed him through the landscape like a shadow. He'd noted that the woman, "Annie," was observant— *too* observant— and intended to keep her as far away from his secrets as possible.

"This is the greenhouse, where we grow fifty percent of our food," Tania said, opening a set of tall, glass doors connected to an enormous greenhouse that butted up to the property.

Banks stepped inside, a dewy chill frosting the skin on his arms. The greenhouse was kept moist by a set of sprinklers that ran across the perimeter of the roof. Rows of wooden planters stood in a line like soldiers, each one labeled according to the type of produce grown within. Cucumbers. Tomatoes. Salad greens.

"We try to meet as many of our own needs as possible, but obviously it's necessary to make trips into town each week," Tania added, looking around the greenhouse with pride. "But we strive every day to be as self-sufficient as possible. By growing produce here, we save not only funds but protect the environment. Mark has helped us foster growing practices that utilize the least amount of energy possible while limiting our carbon footprint."

"It seems like you have a couple of residents who are passionate about the planet," the female detective, Annie, said. Banks couldn't help but think she wasn't sure of that hypothesis at all but was simply fishing for information. He disliked her immediately, and everything she'd done since the moment he'd met her only confirmed his initial impression.

Phony, Banks thought, rolling his eyes.

"Yes," Tania agreed. "Mark's main reason for joining the commune was to be in a place where he was reducing his environmental impact. He's encouraged quite a few of us to be more connected with the planet. Guru Mett has even taken up the cause, and he grows his own little garden outside his bungalow."

"What's in his garden?" Annie asked, curious.

"Well, I supposed, much of what you see here," Tania pointed at a planter box of cucumbers. "He grows vegetables, but some flowers too. Although," she leaned in, shaking her head, "I can't honestly tell you he's as successful with his crops as we are with the greenhouse. Everything he plants seems to die. But he's more about the mental health benefits of gardening than the resulting food supply. He sees it as a strike against capitalism."

"Interesting," Annie said, although Banks didn't see what was interesting about it at all.

Tania turned to Banks, a curious look on her face, as if she noticed his lack of engagement and was bothered by it. "When we sign up for chores, the greenhouse is one of the more popular options."

"Chores," Banks agreed, nodding. "Sounds great. I'll definitely try to get a slot."

"Each week we leave a sign-up sheet for chores in the community room," Tania explained to the group. "Residents can choose what they'd like to do. At first, people tend to sign up for a variety of tasks, but then they end up finding their 'groove' so to speak. We don't have official labels or a hierarchy here, but residents naturally gravitate toward what they like. Mark ends up signing up to go into town with his fancy corn oil truck. Cord always chooses the cleaning and maintenance activities. I tend to choose as many cooking spots as possible." She smiled at Banks as if this was wonderful news. "You'll find your own rhythm, too."

"Awesome," Banks said, trying to appear invested in the idea.

"So, if there's no hierarchy, how do you solve disputes?" Annie asked, her voice piping up from over Banks' shoulder.

"Yeah," her partner Ethan said. "What happens when people disagree on something?"

Tania brought her hands to her chest as if in prayer. "When a dispute arises, we talk it out in a mediated setting. Guru Mett does a lot of the negotiating and leads informal mediated sessions. You'd be surprised, though, how little there is to fight about when you're counting on each other. On that note, let me show you to the meditation area."

Tania motioned for the group to follow her out the back doors of the greenhouse and ushered them down the trail toward the cabins, stopping at the back of a large cabin that belonged to Guru Mett. "Guru Mett paid to have this additional room added to the back of his cabin. It has a separate entrance that anyone is welcome to use." She opened the backdoor, revealing a meditation studio, decorated with pillows, chimes hanging from the ceiling. "Any resident can come to use the space as they please, and Mett holds daily yoga sessions."

"Not to be rude, but— Guru is a Sanskrit term," Ethan said, treading carefully. "But then yoga is an Eastern thing and meditation is Buddhist. So is Guru Mett Hindu, or Buddhist, or— ?"

"Guru Mett is a Guru," Tania shrugged, leaving it at that.

The group followed her past a collection of hot tubs near the base of the mountain. They were scattered behind the bungalows in such a way that each one offered a private retreat. "There's nothing like sitting in the warm water on a cold night, and looking up at the stars," Tania said.

Banks stared at the hot tubs and thought about how different this life was from the one he had left behind. As if she could read his mind, the female detective— Annie— cleared her throat before asking:

"Is this a break from your life before, too?" She was smiling at him as if she understood something secret and special. "Ethan and I came here from a busier background, and it's taken some getting used to. What did you do before joining?

Tania made a *tsk*ing sound. "Remember… we don't talk about the past here."

"That's going to make my investigation rather difficult," Annie said.

"It's our only rule," Tania shrugged in response. "And you will abide by it or leave *Serenity Peaks*."

"It's no problem," Banks said, trying to seem amiable. "I can tell you, without getting into specifics, that this is a welcome change." He winked at Annie, hoping he would seem easy-going. He considered— and hoped— that she might be making up stories about him at this very moment. Good. He wanted to mislead her. Because the truth was, Banks had left a very exciting life behind. One he didn't want Annie to discover.

Later, when the tour was over, Banks retreated to his small, private cabin. He pulled back the curtains and glanced out the window to ensure no one was loitering or spying. When he was sure the coast was clear, he removed his cell phone from its hiding spot in a box on the kitchen counter, then sent a text to an unknown number.

He waited for a response, staring at a series of blinking dots that told him the person on the other end was typing.

Then, the answer came:

Banks bristled in surprise. He was a man with a very specific set of skills, including hand-to-hand combat, shooting with the aim of a sniper, and clean disposal of a body. He wasn't a detective. He hardly had an eye for detail. And now they wanted him to solve the murder of Russel Grey?

This wasn't what he had come here for. He sighed as he stood and walked toward the coffee maker, hitting a button on top after inserting a single K-cup. Every day this job just got increasingly ridiculous. *Figure out who killed him,* Banks thought to himself. They were setting him up to fail— that was the truth. It would take a bevy of skills outside his usual talents to do such a thing. There was a simmering sound as the coffee poured into his cup. Banks took a sip, and the caffeine injection seemed to shake his brain out of its frozen state.

Maybe *he* didn't have the skills to find out who killed Russel Grey. But that Annie woman certainly did. Like many mediocre men before him, Banks committed himself to copying the work of another. He would follow that Annie woman and her partner, piecing together a story from what they discovered.

Banks took the ceramic mug back to the bed with him, then swung his feet over the side. He took another sip before setting the mug on the bedside table, then picked up his phone and answered the message he'd received.

BANKS

I'm on it.

There. It was done. Banks cursed the complexity of the position he'd found himself in, but at least there was one flashing, undeniable bright side:

He would no longer have to use the unregistered, illegally obtained handgun he'd sewn into the lining of his suitcase. Maybe, if he played his cards the right way, he could look at his time at *Serenity Peaks* as a vacation.

"At least there won't be any blood this time," he said out loud to no one in particular. Yes. There wouldn't be any blood. Or at least, he hoped there wouldn't be. If the detective stayed in her lane.

CHAPTER ELEVEN

THERE WAS a creaking sound as Annie and Ethan opened the door to Russel's small bungalow at the edge of the commune, its peaked roof jutting out against the trees that marked the beginning of the forest and the end of the clearing. The exterior of the cabin looked the same as all the others but— as Annie and Ethan soon discovered— the interior of this particular cabin was unique.

"Wow," Ethan said, following Annie into the dark, cramped space and flicking on a light. "I guess the guy really liked... puzzles?"

"And games," Annie agreed.

They looked around the room, taking in the presence of multiple games strewn across the space. On the coffee table sat a partially completed puzzle of a naturescape. On the couch, a stack of childhood favorites, including Clue, Go Fish, and Uno. A partially finished game of Scrabble was situated next to the kitchen sink, and— in the far corner of the room— a bookshelf held stacks of other board games, teetering on top of each other in no discernable pattern.

"In fact," Annie said, stepping deeper into the space, "I think we're in one right now."

"A game?"

"Yes," Annie nodded. "I'm beginning to believe we are moving along a board, perhaps just the way Russel wanted."

"Doubt that," Ethan muttered, picking up a loose bill that had fallen onto the floor from a Monopoly set. "Russel ended up dead, so it looks like he lost."

"Not necessarily," Annie said as she opened a dresser drawer, failing to elaborate further except to say: "It depends on the rules of the game."

Together, the pair searched the space, careful to open every drawer, working meticulously so as not to disturb the area. In the kitchenette, Annie pulled open every drawer on the cabinet, revealing a pleasing scene: spoons, forks, and knives were arranged in an exact order, equal numbers of each. In the lower drawer, canned foods were organized alphabetically. In the top drawer, mixing bowls were organized by size.

"Are you seeing what I'm seeing?" Ethan called out from the closet, where he had opened the doors to reveal shirts organized not just by length, but by color. Beside them, pants hung in a tidy row, arranged in a similar fashion.

"Russel was very organized," Annie said.

"The guy was a nut job," Ethan countered. "Who lives this way? Every drawer is so perfect. It's almost like it was professionally organized."

"No," Annie shook her head. "It's more like…" she paused, trying to find the right comparison. "It's almost like staging a house, or set decoration." She stood, removing her latex gloves and taking in the space. "There's no sign he really *lived* here. Not a dirty mug. Not a piece of lint on the carpet. There's not even any trash in the trashcan." She held up the white bucket can that was positioned in the kitchen, revealing an immaculate, empty tub. "And" she sniffed the air. "Do you smell that?"

"Cleaning fluid," Ethan nodded.

"He scrubbed this place," Annie said, her eyes scanning the room. "He scrubbed it top to bottom and then he staged it, just like you would if you were selling a home."

"What does that mean for us?"

"It means everything we're seeing here was something Russel *wanted* us to see."

"Or something the person who killed him wanted us to see," Ethan suggested.

"Could be," Annie agreed. "But I think he did this himself." She paced around the room, a theory brewing. "I think Russel knew what was coming and he wanted to help us."

"*Help* us?" Ethan scoffed, aghast. "Help us what?"

"Help us solve his murder." Annie moved toward the Scrabble game that had been left out by the kitchen sink, bringing her face eye level to the board, her nose almost touching its edge. "The man leaves nothing in disarray, except for the games strewn across the room. Maybe he hoped I would see the problem— the inconsistency here. He was getting my attention. He was sending us a message."

"Annie," Ethan said gently. "For that to be true he'd have to have known how observant you are. Nobody's brain works like yours."

Annie stared at the letters that had not been used in the Scrabble game. The tiles were positioned in the tiny rectangular holder, their order apparently meaningless.

ANHEINDANETAN

Annie leaned over the tiles, rearranging them into a different order.

"You're right," Annie said. "He knew we were coming." She turned the tile holder toward Ethan. The letters as Annie had rearranged them now read:

ANNIE AND ETHAN

"He's getting our attention," Annie said. "This room is a puzzle box, full of clues. We just have to figure out where to begin."

Ethan joined her beside the Scrabble board, the two of them looking at the words that had already been spelled out, there:

GAME HELLO SUSPECT EACH ISA

"Isa isn't a word," Ethan said. "It's a name."

"Not a name," Annie shook her head. "He combined the words, 'is' and 'a.'" Annie rearranged the words on the board, separating them where they connected to spell a sentence.

HELLO EACH SUSPECT IS A GAME

"Hello, each suspect is a game," Annie read aloud. She turned, scanning the room. "Each game relates to someone who might have killed him." She locked eyes with Ethan, the two of them understanding what this meant.

"Divide and conquer," Annie instructed. "Look for names of members of the commune. He'll have hidden it in the game. We should come up with six."

The pair split up and searched the space, with Ethan the first to find a relevant game. "Pictionary," he said, holding up a flipbook. "To play Pictionary you guess the picture…" Ethan looked at the first sketch in the flipbook. "There's a flower as the first drawing. That has to be Fleur?"

"Pictionary for Fleur," Annie agreed. Across the room, she held up a toy truck that was kept next to a track made from Hot Wheels parts. "The truck," she said, examining it closer. "The name painted on the side is Mark."

"Hot Wheels for Mark," Ethan said, moving on to a game that was situated by the bedside table. It was a square board with four plastic hippos organized around it, their mouths ready to chomp at any moment. "Look at this," he said, plucking a post-it note off the top and reading the message scrawled on its face. "It says, 'Tania: How we hATE the games we play. The a-t-e are capitalized."

"Ate," Annie nodded. "And they're hippos that eat the balls. Hungry Hippos for Tania, then."

"Monopoly for Guru Mett," Ethan leaned over the coffee table, pointing at a Monopoly game that had been left in progress. "You won't believe this one." He held up one of the fake dollar bills: a striking likeness of Guru Mett had been printed on the front of the bill.

"Clever," Annie nodded. "Monopoly for the Guru. That just leaves—"

"Cord and Banks," Ethan said. "I've got Cord," he said, leading Annie toward the open clothes closet. There, positioned on a shelf next to folded sweaters, was an active game of *Sorry*. "He left a Cord wrapped on top," Ethan shrugged, holding up a cut piece of woven cord. "I thought it was weird when I was looking at the clothes."

"That's *Sorry* for Cord. Which just leaves Banks," Annie said, her mind reeling, flipping through images of the space. "There was something—" She stopped mid-sentence, heading back into the kitchen, Ethan on her heel. She led them to a little round dining room table, where a game of Connect Four stood in-progress. Annie leaned over it, taking in the red and blue chips. She ripped a post-it note off the top. It read, simply:

> *THE NEWEST ONE WILL CONNECT*
> *FOUR YOU.*

"Connect four," Annie said. "The newest one is Banks. He got here right before the murder. Russel must have known a new member was on the way."

"Makes sense," Ethan agreed. He glanced down at his

notes, summarizing what he'd written. "So, we have *Pictionary* for Fleur. *Hot Wheels* for Mark. *Hungry Hippos* for Tania. *Monopoly* for Guru Mett. *Sorry* for Cord. And *Connect Four* for Banks. Any idea what it all means?"

Annie bent down to the level of the Connect Four game, the red and blue chips reminding her of the colors of police lights and ambulances. "I have a suspicion," she said. "But I'd like to make it a fact." Annie scanned the rest of the games, stopping at the Hungry Hippo board that had been earmarked for Tania. She let her fingers skim the top of one of the plastic animals, stopping when she noticed something caught in its jaw. She plucked it from the creature's teeth, turning it over in her fingers:

It was a dried piece of a plant, its brush-like tendrils ending in the tiniest purple flowers.

Annie stood, wiping her hands on her jeans. "I'll need to speak to the residents. Let's start with Tania," Annie smiled. "She's been such a gracious host, after all."

CHAPTER TWELVE

TANIA

TANIA'S HANDS shook as she turned on the tea kettle in her tiny bungalow. It was an electric kettle and only required the flip of a switch to operate, but— with two detectives seated at the table behind her— Tania found that the motion took more effort than usual. She cleared her throat, turning around and offering the pair a smile.

"Two chamomile teas, fresh from the garden," she said, passing them the mugs.

Annie peered down the open mouth of her glass, looking at the strainer within. A dried collection of flowers and leaves stared back at her, nestled between mesh wire that settled the tincture in the warm water.

"You even grow your own tea here?" Annie asked, curious.

"We attempt to do as much as we can on our own," Tania answered, taking a seat at the table. "Our goal has always been to create a self-sustaining community that can hold its own. But still, the occasional trip to the store doesn't hurt." She winked at Annie.

"What's the point of that?" Ethan asked, taking a sip of his tea. "I mean, why care so much about not being dependent on the rest of the world?"

Tania nodded, setting down her cup. "The thing is, here at *Serenity Peaks*, we believe people are fundamentally good. Especially when they live in small villages, families, and communities, which is what was always intended. Think about Native American tribes and indigenous cultures. They formed small societies of a few dozen families that could be self-sustaining without destroying the land. But society as a whole—" Tania waved a hand in the air. "It's gotten too big. Too unwieldy. The sheer size of it all is to blame for so many of life's problems. When people get together in large groups, society becomes a machine in which there are winners and losers. Here at *Serenity Peaks*, we keep the community small enough that we can run it through cooperation. This is truly how human beings were meant to live."

"How do you fund the thing?" Ethan asked.

"When members join, they make a one-time cash donation. Guru Mett keeps the financial records for us, but overall, our operating cost is quite low. We try to do as much of the maintenance work ourselves as possible."

"I can see that," Annie agreed, privately thinking she'd noticed that the roof on their own bungalow featured uneven shingles and had clearly not been installed by a professional. "How did you come into owning the property?"

"We actually all own it together," Tania answered. "When someone buys into the commune, their name is added to the trust that manages the estate. I simply serve as the functioning power of attorney when making big decisions. The founder of the commune put the orders in his will upon his death."

"Were you close to him?"

"He was like a father to me," Tania said. "All my life I'd been wandering. He created a place I felt at home." She glanced up, taking in their expressions and seeing something there that was familiar, and infuriating. "I know what you're thinking," she sighed, rolling her eyes. "But *Serenity Peaks* isn't and hasn't ever been that 'type' of commune."

"No, of course not—" Annie offered

"I wasn't thinking anything—" Ethan started to say.

"It's fine," Tania laughed. "People hear the word commune and they assume it's a cult dedicated to one creepy leader or that everyone is sleeping together. That's never happened here. This is just a place for people to come and live in community with each other. Think of it as the TV Show *Friends*. We're just good neighbors who choose to live away from the isolation of the outside world. Isn't it funny people move to cities where there's millions of other humans, but they sit in a tiny apartment alone, and walk on crowded street corners feeling like they don't know anyone?"

"It is," Annie said, understanding what she meant.

"Well, that doesn't happen here. We try to really get to know each other and provide support. The only rule is not to talk about our past lives."

"Why not?" Ethan countered. "To really know someone don't you have to know where they come from?"

Tania stirred some honey into her tea, her spoon clanking against the ceramic mug. "To be honest, we get some residents who have had quite traumatic pasts. The rule was put in place to help them feel this is a chance to start over. If they choose to volunteer details here and there, that's fine. But we want people to form a new identity that allows them to be free."

"So, you didn't know anything about Russel's past?" Annie asked. "I know it's against the rule to bring it up, but it could be key in trying to figure out what happened to him."

"All I know is that Russel left a bad situation," Tania shrugged. "He showed up here years ago with nothing but a pile of cash. He was quite upset. He'd driven that truck that now belongs to Mark Wayans. Mark's done it up to make it environmentally friendly of course."

"The truck was Russel's first?" Annie confirmed.

"Yes, he shared it with Mark, some deal between the two of them."

"So he was upset that night?"

"He simply told me he wanted to join. He said his name was Russel, although I can't even be sure of that because some people— those fleeing a difficult situation— often change their names when they arrive. He gave me the money and I welcomed him to our collective. Every day since, he proved himself to be an asset to the community."

"He was?"

"Oh yes. A model citizen. He helped every person here. Formed connections. Took every chore seriously. He organized game nights with all of us."

"Was there a specific game you played with him?" Annie asked.

"I always beat him at Hungry Hippos." A smile crossed Tania's eyes at the memory. "Russel was committed to this place." She paused, inhaling deeply. "He will be missed."

Seeing that she had upset Tania, Annie stood, motioning for Ethan to follow her. "Thank you for talking to us. We'll just be on our way."

Tania led them to the door. As she opened it, Annie stepped onto the wrap- around porch, noting the planter boxes there. "This is where you grow your tea?"

Tania bristled. "Yes. Chamomile. Lavender."

"And this one?" Annie stopped at an empty planter box, soil that had recently been churned within.

"Oh, that one just got pruned," Tania said casually. "Afraid it didn't make it, poor thing."

Annie reached into the dirt, digging a little. Under her fingers, tiny brown, dried leaves appeared, flowers at the tip in just the faintest shade of purple.

"What plant was it?" Annie asked again.

There was a long pause as Tania considered her answer.

"Lupine," she said, knowing as she heard the words come out of her mouth that she should have lied. Instead, she told the truth. And she suspected it might cost her everything. "I take it to sleep. It helps— with insomnia."

"Lupine," Annie nodded. "Thank you for your time."

With that, Annie and Ethan disappeared down the stairs and around the trail, leaving Tania alone on the porch, considering what was a lie and what was the truth, and if the difference between the two mattered much at all.

CHAPTER THIRTEEN

GURU METT

GURU METT WAS SEATED in the meditation room, his legs crossed on a pillow, eyes shut tight. In the background, a C.D. of wind instruments played, offering a soothing tone. Although technology wasn't technically allowed at *Serenity Peaks*, Guru Mett had convinced Tania to make an exception in the case of the music for his meditation classes, given the health benefits such healing offered to residents. Of course, the two new residents seated in front of him were of a different kind. Guru Mett opened one of his eyes, risking a peek at his guests.

In front of him, Annie and Ethan sat on two plush pillows, their legs crossed, eyes closed.

"And now," Guru Mett continued his meditation speech. "Imagine the thoughts that bother you caught up in a stream. Place those thoughts gently on the water. Watch as the current takes them away."

The man— Ethan— shifted. Guru Mett could sense he wasn't comfortable with meditation. Too many people were bothered by being alone with their thoughts.

"The current takes them down the stream, bringing them

away from the banks and dry land. The thoughts get smaller and smaller as they're removed from your view—"

Ethan shifted again, a small smile crossing his face. Beside him, Annie kept her eyes shut tight, apparently very focused on the exercise.

"Ethan?" Guru Mett said, a little annoyed. "Do you want to share the visual you've created?"

"Sure," Ethan said, his eyes still shut tight. "My thoughts are in a giant blue dumpster bin. The kind you find on city street corners. They're all shoved in there in enormous trash bags and the whole thing is lit on fire. It's floating down the river, an enormous trash can fire of distress."

There was a long silence, and the woman— Annie— let a smile cross her face. Guru Mett sighed. Some people just couldn't be helped.

"Good enough," Guru Mett said, ready to give up entirely. "Start to bring awareness back into your body. Wiggle your fingers, your toes. And when you're ready— slowly open your eyes."

Annie opened her eyes, staring at Guru Mett with a bright curiosity that never seemed to dim. Ethan stretched his arms toward the ceiling, a yawn echoing across the space. "That was great," Ethan said. "Really helpful. I feel so much more relaxed, thank you."

"You're welcome," Guru Mett offered a half-bow, hands in prayer position. "I just thought it would be best to ground ourselves before we get into questions. It's always better to approach things from a place of balance." Fifteen minutes ago, Annie and Ethan had knocked on his door to question him about the death of Russel Grey, and Guru Mett had redirected them into a meditation. A small part of him had hoped his exercise would lull them into sleep, but of course, they both looked more alert than ever.

"We really appreciate you taking the time to meet with us,"

Annie began, smiling at him as if she meant no harm, when Guru Mett was quite sure that she did. "What happened to Russel was really awful."

"Yes," Guru Mett agreed. "Nothing like that has ever happened here in *Serenity Peaks*."

"That's what's so curious about it, isn't it?" Annie asked. "That's why I don't believe that *Serenity Peaks* was a factor. It wasn't the location that led to Russel's death. This wasn't a random act of crime."

"Yes?" Guru Mett leaned in, intrigued by her theory. "If that's the case, then what was the key factor?

"I can't be sure," Annie said. "It could have been someone with a vendetta. Or maybe...

"Maybe?"

"Maybe it was something to do with Russel's past," Annie continued. "Something from his life before he moved here that came back to bite him. The problem is there's a rule in *Serenity Peaks* about not discussing the past. Which, you can imagine, makes it difficult for me to get to the bottom of things. If nobody knows what Russel's life was like before he moved here, how am I to piece the puzzle together?"

"Yes," Guru Mett nodded. "That does present quite the problem."

"So on that note... did Russel ever mention anything about his past to you?"

Guru Mett shook his head. "Never. Although," he paused. "I did get the impression he was running from something. The residents here come and go in terms of attending my yoga sessions and meditation classes. But Russel? He attended religiously. Never missed a single session up until he died. I think it gave him peace to visit me. I got the sense he was trying to exorcise some kind of demon within, or atone for his life before, or perhaps to just find some way to mentally leave it all behind. *Serenity Peaks* appeals to people who want to forget where they came from." Guru Mett paused, thinking about his own reasons for coming to *Serenity Peaks*. He'd also been escaping the past. His musings weren't lost on Annie, who seemed to sense how he felt.

"And why did you come to *Serenity Peaks?*" She asked, not a hint of accusation in her voice. Even so, Guru Mett bristled.

"To help others," he said, motioning around the studio. "This is a place where I can focus full-time on being of service through spiritual practice."

"That makes sense," Annie agreed. She stood, stretching her legs and reaching toward the ceiling. "Thank you for your time." Her partner followed her, the two of them making their way toward the door.

"That's it?" Guru Mett asked, a little surprised. He'd been expecting more of an inquisition. "No other questions."

"Not for now," Annie shrugged casually, as if something had slipped her mind. "Oh, maybe one!" She clapped her hands together, pleased with herself. "Did you ever go to Russel's game nights?"

"We played a few times," Guru Mett answered, unsure why any of this was important. "He was quite the lover of puzzles. Games aren't as much my joy."

"Is there any reason he'd leave a game behind for you?"

Guru Mett's eyes widened in surprise. This was news to him— and concerning news at that. "What game?"

"Monopoly," Annie said. "We found something that made us believe he wanted you to have the game. Monopoly."

Guru Mett's heart quickened, but he tried not to let his expression shift. He thought about the computer under the floorboard of this very room, hiding in the dark of a nook that could be so easily discovered by others. "Monopoly? That's strange. We never played it together. I honestly have no idea."

Annie nodded as if his assurances were enough for her. "Thank you for your time," she said. And with that, they headed for the door.

Guru Mett's entire body relaxed once the pair was gone.

What a terrible mess he'd found himself in. And it all came back to that laptop— the one he *should* destroy but couldn't, given that he'd made a promise to an old friend. A promise that was becoming increasingly difficult to keep.

CHAPTER FOURTEEN

FLEUR

FLEUR'S CABIN was covered in art. It was tiny and bright, just like her.

Fleur had never been good with people. Even as a child, she had preferred to be alone with her markers and pens. She was a quiet soul who retreated into art to avoid the worst of life— but somehow, the worst of life seemed to follow her anyway.

"You shouldn't poke around in all this," Fleur said to Annie and Ethan, who were seated at the coffee table in her little cabin at *Serenity Peaks*. Fleur hadn't offered them anything to drink, because she was hoping they wouldn't stay long. "What happened to Russel, I mean."

"And why's that?" Annie said brightly, folding her hands on the table. "The definition of a detective is someone who pokes around in things." She looked about the room, noticing the sketches hanging from the walls. There were hand-drawn images of plants and animals common to the area— wild stags and doe-eyed deer. But what interested Annie was the drawings of familiar people. An image of a woman that resembled Tania, sitting on a fallen log. A drawing of a man who looked like Russel, standing in front of a bevy of computers. Everyone in the commune was represented in some way or another.

"Because," Fleur answered. "You just shouldn't. It's better to leave bad things alone."

"You're quite the artist," Annie said, nodding at the images on the wall.

Fleur shrugged her shoulders. "It's just what I've always done. Drawing is the only thing that makes sense sometimes."

"What brought you to *Serenity Peaks?*" Annie asked, eliciting a horrified expression from Fleur.

"We don't talk about the past here," Fleur said, rocking back and forth a little in her chair.

"That doesn't mean you can't tell me what brought you here," Annie shrugged as if the matter was not an important one at all. "Without getting into specifics of course."

"I came because I wanted to be free," Fleur answered. "You'd be surprised how hard that is out there." She nodded out the window, indicating the outside world.

"Yes," Annie agreed. "Nobody is really free, are they?"

"Not from money," Fleur answered. "Not from time. Not from struggle. No, nobody is really free."

"How well did you know Russel?" Annie asked.

Fleur felt her throat tighten at the mention of Russel's name. She remembered her last conversation with him. What he had wanted her to do. But her arms trembled at the thought. Without her permission, her body began to tighten, her fists clenching into balls. "Not well," Fleur lied, her voice sounding too high- pitched and far away.

"Did you ever play board games with him?" Annie asked.

"Yes."

"What did you play?"

"Pictionary," Fleur answered, her voice barely a whisper. "But it doesn't matter now."

"No," Annie shook her head, leaning in and looking at Fleur as if she could see straight through her. "Don't you see?"

She reached out and touched Fleur's hand. "It matters now more than ever. He left it for you, you know. The game? He marked Pictionary for you. I wonder why?" There was a moment where the two of them seemed to speak without words, and then Annie stood, signaling it was time to leave. "Ethan and I will come back. When you're ready."

With that, they left Fleur to herself, with nothing but the pictures on her wall.

CHAPTER FIFTEEN

MARK

MARK WAS INSTALLING solar panels on the roof of his cabin when Annie and Ethan stopped by to ask him questions about Russel.

"Hope you don't mind if I keep working on the panels!" Mark called down from on top of the roof of his cabin. Beneath him, Annie and Ethan craned their necks to look upwards, trying to make out his shape as he moved from the shade toward the sun.

"No problem," Annie called back, keeping one hand over her eyes to shield her face from the glare. "Tania mentioned you were close with Russel."

There was a pounding sound as Mark nailed a connective piece onto the roof. "As close as anybody," he said, his voice covered by the sound of the hammer so that Annie and Ethan were forced to lean in to hear him. "Russel was a foundational member of the group in a way. Besides Tania, he'd been here the longest. He made an effort to get to know everyone."

Mark wiped his brow, hoping he'd distanced himself from appearing to have any sort of special connection with Russel. He glanced down at Annie. She looked exactly like her photograph. Mark hated that he knew what she looked like before she'd even arrived. It made him feel dirty, almost criminal. Like the person he'd been before he arrived in *Serenity Peaks* —the person he'd tried to leave behind.

Damnit, Russel, he thought to himself. *What the hell did you get me into?*

He moved to another panel and pulled out an electric drill, creating a hole to secure the solar battery into place. Mark was secretly hoping the act of being in construction would keep the two detectives away from him. Maybe all the noise would create enough frustration that they'd give up the interview and move on to someone else.

"What kind of person did you find Russel to be?" Annie called over the sound of the drill, relentless in her pursuit of the truth. "How would you describe him?"

Mark stopped drilling and set the power tool down. He sat back on his heels, breathless, wiping the sweat from his forehead. "He was methodical," Mark said, shaking his head. "He liked to line up all the pieces to solve a problem and knock 'em down as he went."

"And what about you?" Annie said, stepping forward. "You moved here for the environmental impact, correct? You wanted to live with a lower carbon footprint."

"That's right," Mark agreed. "Just wanted to do my part for the environment."

"And prior to this you worked on environmental programs?"

Mark paused, then climbed down the ladder that led to the roof, finally meeting Annie and Ethan on the porch. He removed his gloves, resting them on the banister.

"You know, round here they really prefer we don't talk about the past. Gives us the chance to start fresh."

"And that's what you were looking for? A fresh start?" Annie asked.

"Sometimes a person needs that," Mark answered, a faraway look in his eyes. "A person needs to go somewhere they can live their truth. That's why I came to *Serenity Peaks*. To live my truth."

"Are you living it now?"

Mark didn't respond. Instead, he answered Annie's question only with silence, letting the moment hang heavy in the air.

Ethan broke the spell. "Your truck," he said, pointing at the pick-up truck that was parked in front of Mark's cabin. "How long have you had it?"

"Over a decade," Mark shrugged. "It's an old thing but I rigged it to run on corn oil. Better for the planet than gasoline. It's my baby."

"Have you been in it since Russel's death?" Annie asked, arching an eyebrow.

"Why would that matter?"

"I was just wondering if you'd searched the truck," Annie continued, her mind remembering the Hot Wheels version of the truck she'd found earlier, with Mark's name painted on the side. "If Russel knew it was important, maybe he would have left you something there."

"You make it sound like he knew he was going to die," Mark said without a hint of surprise in his voice.

"Just a suspicion," Annie shrugged. "Not a fact." She glanced up at the solar panels on the roof. "We'll leave you to it. Thanks for taking the time."

With that, Annie and Ethan took their leave. Mark put his gloves back on and headed up the ladder, thinking about what Annie had said, a terrible feeling in the pit of his stomach.

———

Later, when he was sure the coast was clear and the two detectives were well away from his cabin, Mark climbed down from the roof. A sense of urgency drove him forward, his legs moving of their own accord. The female detective's words replayed on his mind in a loop.

Maybe he would have left you something there.

It was true. Before his death, Russel had given Mark explicit instructions on what to do with the truck. Instructions Mark had— so far— continued to resist. Technically, the truck still belonged to Russel. But it had been Mark's de facto vehicle for so many years, and he had poured so much love and care into it that he couldn't imagine living without it.

Almost in the way he couldn't imagine living without Russel.

This truck was the last piece of Russel that Mark had left. And Russel had asked him to give it away. It was a special kind of cruelty that made Mark's cheeks flush with rage.

But now, there was another possibility. *What if Russel had left him something in the truck?*

Mark's mind raced as he approached the driver's side, unlocking the vehicle with a familiar gold key. The truck was old enough that it didn't have auto locks, and Mark liked it that way. It was old, and set in its way, a stubborn mule of a thing, just like him— and just like Russel.

The door opened with a satisfying click and Mark hopped inside to begin the search. He hoped to find a letter. Or something meaningful. At first, his search yielded no price, but then he opened the glovebox.

What he found within was like a punch to the face. It wasn't a letter.

It was a map. And— judging by the location that was circled on the map's face— this route wasn't meant for Mark at all.

It was meant for the person Russel wanted the truck to go to. Mark was under explicit instructions that he was currently disobeying. He was to give the truck to the individual Russel had specified. Mark hadn't understood the reason for the request at the time— but now, after finding this map— the reason was clear.

Russel, Mark shook his head, *what have you gotten us into?*

Mark paused to consider his next steps, then, he put the map back in the glovebox and slammed it shut, locking it so that no one would find what was within.

CHAPTER SIXTEEN

CORD

CORD WAS SERVICING one of *Serenity Peaks'* many hot tubs when Annie and Ethan came to interview him. He held the edge of a long net on a handle, using it to scrape leaves from the bubbling water below. The hot tub was positioned on a wooden platform, and a bag filled with chemicals sat by Cord's feet. A PH adjuster. Chlorine. All of it at the ready, along with a manual on how to use test trips to gauge the water's needs.

"I like to keep things right," Cord said to Annie and Ethan, who were standing in front of him down the steps that led to the jacuzzi. "Nobody else even volunteers for my chores anymore because they know I like 'em and I'm the best at 'em."

"I can see that," Annie said, watching as Cord bent down to the chemicals at his feet and threw a tablet in the bubbling water. "What do you like most about living here?"

"The thing about a commune is it's how people are meant to be," Cord shrugged, sharing something he'd thought about often. "Out there," he looked at the horizon, "I was all alone. Nobody really owed me anything, and I didn't owe them nothing either. See, besides family, and sometimes even with 'em, people out there live all alone. In a big city, you could fall on the street and people would walk by, think you were homeless or strung out on drugs. They wouldn't even stop to help you. And even if you *are* homeless or on drugs, they should stop. But they don't." Cord leaned on the edge of the hot tub, shaking his head. "Don't you think that's strange?"

"I guess it is," Ethan agreed, nodding. "We get used to walking past people."

"It never made sense to me," Cord said, his face childlike and open. The way he spoke made Annie think he might be on the spectrum. He struggled to make eye contact, and shuffled his energy back and forth, making him rock side to side. "I kept trying to help everybody out there and they looked at me like I was crazy. Ended up getting taken advantage of most of the time when all I really wanted was to make friends."

"Is that what brought you to *Serenity Peaks*?" Annie asked.

"It's a long story," Cord said. "But my family didn't like me all that much. So, I left when I was fourteen. Bounced around on the street. Met all kinds of people— some of them real good. Some of them not so much. I hitchhiked around and someone left me off at the town at the base of the mountain. That's where I met Tania. She was doing a grocery run and she took me in."

"Did you have to pay the initiation fee?" Annie asked, curious.

"Oh sure," Cord nodded seriously. "It was a big commitment. Tania took almost half my money."

"And how much was that?" Ethan asked, concerned.

"Five dollars," Cord said solemnly.

Annie's mouth dropped open. "Cord," she shook her head. "Did you know that other residents paid a one-time fee of ten thousand dollars or more to be here?"

"Dunno," Cord said, scratching his chin. "Tania told me the

fee just had to feel big enough to the person that they felt invested in the community. Guess for me, five dollars was a big investment at the time. It was almost all the money in my pocket."

"Makes sense," Annie smiled at him. "And you like it here?"

"I do," Cord said eagerly. "It was like I was saying. People weren't meant to live alone and not owe each other anything. Ancient humans lived in small villages, didn't they? Russel gave me a book about it when I first moved here. Took me some time to work through it, but it made me realize that I wasn't the weird one for wanting to help others. All that time I was out on the street, I'd get in trouble. I'd share my last dime with the stranger in the tent next to me, and he'd take off with it. I'd loan someone my bicycle and they'd never come back. I was starting to think I was the dumb one, or the crazy one for trusting people, but then Russel gave me this book on villages, and it all made sense. *I wasn't* the weird one for caring about people. I was just needin' to be in a village. Where everyone else cares, too. You see?"

"I do," Annie told Cord, watching as he turned off the hot tub's jets and pulled the lid over the top to protect it. "Were you close with Russel?"

"It's weird you said '*were,*'" Cord's face flushed and he pulled at his collar. "It still feels like he's here to me."

"I know," Annie said sadly. "It does feel that way."

"We were close. He gave me books and talked to me about things. Like a Dad would do. We played board games."

"What did you play?" Annie said, her eyes lighting up.

"All kinds of things," Cord answered. "Every board game you can imagine."

"Cord," Annie walked up the steps, putting a hand on his shoulder. "What if I told you that Russel earmarked a certain game for you before he died. Would it mean anything?"

"Depends on the game."

"It was *Sorry*," Annie said, scanning his face for any sign of recognition. Cord's eyes widened and he put a hand to his temple.

"Oh no," he said, shaking his head. "Oh no, oh no, oh no..."

"Cord," Annie whispered, comforting him as best she could. "It's okay. Don't cry. Take a deep breath. Stay with me."

Tears ran down Cord's cheeks and his breathing quickened. "I never meant to hurt anybody," he said. "I never meant to."

"That's okay," Annie answered, her tone smooth like honey. "But Russel would want you to be honest, right?"

"Always."

"He would want you to tell the truth about what you're *Sorry* for. I promise you; I'll do my best to protect you. But you have to be the man Russel wanted you to be."

There was a long moment where Cord scanned Annie's face, wondering if he could trust her. His mind rifled through images of people from his past— those he'd met on the street. A bevy of images played in his mind's eye, all of them whispers of ghosts he'd long forgotten. Cord had trusted the wrong people again and again, until he'd found his village. Now, Russel had left him with a challenge. And, to complete it, he'd need to make another leap of faith into the arms of the woman in front of him.

"Come by my cabin tonight," Cord said, wiping his nose on his sleeve. "My chores are done at eight. I'll show you everything then." There was a resigned weight to his voice, like he knew his world was ending and it was all he could do to sit and watch the sun explode.

"Good man," Annie said, patting his shoulder. "We'll see you tonight." She descended down the stairs, her shoes crunching over leaves as she pulled Ethan away from the hot tub, leaving behind a distressed young man in her wake.

"Sure, it's smart to leave him?" Ethan whispered in her ear, concerned. "He could be a flight risk."

"That boy?" Annie laughed at the idea. "He wouldn't know where to run to."

CHAPTER SEVENTEEN

BANKS

BANKS HAD BEEN TAILING Annie and Ethan all day. At least, he had followed the pair as much as he could, without being discovered. He'd trailed them through their interviews under the guise of doing chores. He carried firewood in from the woods, allowing him to linger outside the meditation room attached to the back of Guru Mett's cottage. He'd watched as they stood outside Mark's cabin, only to notice Mark emerge once they were out of sight and head straight to his truck, a sense of urgency in his step. Banks had watched as Mark opened the glovebox, spotting something there and locking it back inside.

Now, the sun had set, and Banks was clothed in a black hoodie and jeans, a black scarf covering his face as he stood in the clearing outside Mark's cottage. He'd waited until cover of darkness to make his move, sure that he would be able to find what he needed without being discovered.

He approached the place where Mark's white pickup truck sat, grabbing a screwdriver and a hammer to break into the passenger-side door. With force, he managed to pop the lock open, then did the same with the glove box. Foolish of Mark to assume locks could stop any decent tradesman.

Banks reached inside and pulled out the item Mark had locked within. It was a paper map, but not just any map— someone had drawn on its surface in red marker, showing a route from *Serenity Peaks* to another location, which was circled and indicated by latitude and longitude.

Banks considered his options, then removed a lighter from his pocket. Thankfully, he enjoyed the odd cigarette now and then, and while it was ordinarily a habit that caused him quite a bit of trouble, in this moment— it was proving useful.

With a flick of his thumb, the lighter roared to life. Banks held it to the edge of the map, which was eaten up by the flame. The orange tiger climbed its way up the side of the map, until it eventually devoured it whole. Bank dropped the final edge as the fire finished its job, looking down at the scattered ashes on the floor. The map was destroyed. Unreadable. That was all Banks needed.

He jumped down from the passenger side and closed the door softly, not bothering to attempt to cover up the evidence of his destruction. Then, he ran into the night, taking a roundabout route back to his own cabin that led him first into the forest— just to offer plausible deniability in case anyone had seen him. In the woods, he stripped off the hoodie and dropped the handkerchief, revealing a plain t-shirt underneath. Then, he headed back toward the mountain, finally making his way up the dirt road to his little bungalow.

He stepped inside and turned on a lamp on the bedside table, rifling through a drawer to pull out his cellphone. He opened it, speed-dialing a number he hated to call.

"We have a bigger problem than we thought," Banks said as soon as he heard a greeting from the voice on the other end of the line. "I know how he died. He tried to leave them a map."

A shiver ran down Banks' spine as he thought about what this meant. Annie and Ethan had better stop snooping— they were heading down a road that didn't offer U-turns, and the worst was yet to come.

CHAPTER EIGHTEEN

CORD

AT TEN PAST EIGHT, Annie and Ethan stood at the door to Cord's small cabin, a basket of muffins from the community dining hall in Annie's arms.

"We really need to bribe him with food?" Ethan said, eyeing the basket.

"I felt bad we rocked him too hard this morning," Annie countered. "Kid needs a break."

"Unless he's the killer."

"Even killers need carbs," Annie joked. Then, she reached up and knocked on the door. Without delay, Cord answered, ushering them into his small cabin.

"I don't have a lot. Place isn't fancy," he said, looking uncomfortable as he motioned for them to sit at a quaint table in the corner. It was flat and wooden, marks carved into its side. One leg was a little shorter than the other, but Cord had stuck some ticky-tacky underneath to build it up.

"I love what you've done with it," Annie said, smiling. "We've had the great privilege of entering a few cabins here, and every single one is immaculate and unique."

"It's simple," Cord nodded. "But there's something special about living that way."

Annie placed the basket of muffins on the table. "We brought you a snack," she offered. Cord took a muffin from the basket and bit into it without hesitation.

"Did you also bring the game?" Cord said, mouth full.

Ethan nodded, reaching into the duffel bag he'd brought with him. He unzipped the opening and pulled out the game of *Sorry*, leaving it on the table. Cord ran his hands over the surface of the box as if it were something mystical.

"We played all the time," Cord said, his eyes shining. "Russel and me. It made me think of how they show family game nights in commercials. You ever seen those? The advertisement'll be for anything. Even something unrelated. Dish soap. Pizza delivery. But there's this happy family in the living room having a game night. I always wanted a family like that, and when I went to Russel's cabin for game night it felt like I had one."

"Did the other members of the commune join you guys?" Annie asked.

"Sometimes," Cord said, swallowing another bite of his muffin. "But I liked to play more often than them. They'd come about once a week, and we'd all do a night together. But sometimes I'd get bored or lonely and Russel was always up for a game."

"That's nice," Annie said, nodding. "Now... I think you know what I have to ask."

Cord sighed. Then, he stood, walking into the bathroom. He disappeared for a moment, grabbing items off the sink. Then, he returned to the table and spread the items on its surface.

An earring. A scarf. A pencil. A badge.

"What am I looking at?" Ethan said, confused. "This— I thought this was a confession to murder, not a thrift store visit."

Annie elbowed Ethan in the ribs, but the damage was

done. Cord's mouth dropped open. "*Murder?!*" he exclaimed. "Hey, I didn't kill nobody— "

"Of course you didn't," Annie said, shaking her head. "You'll have to excuse my partner. He was confused. Now— the items?"

Cord looked at the floor, suddenly very interested in his shoelaces. "The thing about me is, I got sticky fingers."

"Sticky fingers?" Ethan asked.

"I steal things sometimes. The thing you gotta know is it's not for the money, though!" Cord held up his hands as if he were being arrested. "It's harmless, really. Just something I did as a kid because my parents would leave for a few weeks at a time. And before they went, I would take something out of their bag just to have. Became kind of a habit."

"A habit you kept as you grew up," Annie nodded.

"Right," Cord answered. "Even on the street. I'd meet someone new and like 'em, but I started to learn it'd only be a matter of time before they screwed me over, stole my stuff, or left me. So, before they got the chance to do it, I'd take something of theirs. Not as revenge," he shrugged his shoulders up and down. "Just to remember them by. So I could still have a piece of them with me."

"And these items?" Annie gestured at the table. "Where are they from?"

"Well, that's the bad part," Cord said. "They're from people here at the commune. I've grown real close to everyone and I think they're all staying but on the off chance they leave me one day, now I've got something of theirs to keep. Half of 'em don't even know something's missing. It's easy to get stuff too, because I do so much maintenance in everybody's cabins."

"That makes sense," Annie agreed, trying not to look at Ethan, who had arched his eyebrows as if to say it made no sense whatsoever. "And Russel— did he know you had this habit?"

"I told him once while we were playing a game of *Sorry*," Cord said, hanging his head low. "The title of the game made me feel real guilty about it all, so I told Russel everything. He was real nice about it. I was worried he wouldn't want to hang out with me anymore once he knew but he said he didn't care. He said everyone is a little different and I shouldn't feel bad. That I'm just dealing with the world as best I can. But he also said I should give the stuff back. Not immediately but at the right time.

"At the right time?"

"Yes. Russel told me I should wait until the proper moment, but at the right time I should give it all back and say *Sorry*. He told me it was like the game. That timing is everything. That's why when you said he marked the game for me, I knew— he was telling me that it's time to own up to what I did and say *sorry*."

"Cord," Annie said, scooting forward so she was perched on the edge of her chair. "I'm going to ask you something important. Did you take anything from Russel? Maybe in the days preceding his death?"

"How did you know?" Cord asked, his cheeks turning a brilliant shade of burgundy. "I didn't mean to, but he *knew* I had this problem and he left it out anyway, clear as day on the table. He got up to go to the bathroom and he left it there right in front of me. I half-thought he'd notice it was gone when he got back but he didn't because he was so involved in the game."

"What did you take, Cord?"

Cord reached into the pile on the table and pulled out a white badge. On the front was a simple set of letters spelling out a word: ACCESS, with Russel's name typed above it. On the back was a black strip, indicating the badge could be used in a strip reader. Cord passed the badge to Annie, who held it in her hands like it was something precious.

"I don't know what it goes to," Cord said, a note of caution in his voice. "I'd never seen Russel carry it before that game night. He was wearing it around his neck on a lanyard, then he took it off and set it down. And, well, sticky fingers," Cord held up his hands, wiggling his fingers in the air. "I wish I knew what it went to."

"If you'll let me hold onto it," Annie said, "I might be able to figure that out. Deal? I'll take the badge, and you can have the game." She slid to game of *Sorry* across the table.

"And the muffins," Cord said, pulling the basket of muffins closer to him.

"Of course," Annie said, standing. Ethan followed, and the two of them made their way toward the door. "And Cord— thank you for being honest. I know Russel would be proud of you."

With that, they left a satisfied Cord behind them, gently closing the door to his cabin and immersing themselves in the brisk, night air. They descended down the steps, pine needles crunching beneath their shoes.

"Guess you were right about the muffins," Ethan joked, elbowing Annie lightly. "What do you think it goes to?" He asked, nodding at the badge Annie held in her hands with all the care one would give to a prized possession.

"I'm not sure yet," Annie said, mulling over ideas. "But one thing I'm certain of— Russel wanted Cord to take it. And maybe, just maybe, he wanted us to have it, too."

CHAPTER NINETEEN

MARK

THE COOL EVENING air slid down Mark's throat as he headed for his truck, pulling his jacket tighter around his shoulders. It was a warm, fluffy coat made from environmentally friendly goose-down substitute, and it was supposed to keep Mark warm even under the toughest of conditions. But tonight, the coat wasn't working. Mark felt a chill under his skin that came from somewhere inside him. It was guilt, perhaps, for failing to honor Russel's final wish.

I should tell them about the map, he thought to himself, a shiver running down his spine. He remembered the moments he'd spent with Russel since his arrival. Hours they'd shared together fishing at the lake. Slow, steady hikes through the forest, the two of them picking up leaves to compare. In a place like *Serenity Peaks*, there wasn't much to do. It was the people you were surrounded by that made the land feel like home. And Russel was the first person who had made Mark feel at home.

Mark headed toward his truck, eager to prepare for tonight's festivities. The Commune was holding a surprise event organized by Tania, who thought the group could use a boost. Mark was the only resident who was in on Tania's secret party plans, and he had been tasked with making a quick trip into town to pick up some supplies. As usual, he was running behind schedule.

Mark stopped at the door to his truck, then froze, his breath catching in his throat as he noticed something strange about the passenger side. The glovebox hung wide open, reminding Mark of a jaw dropped in surprise. Its lock had been smashed in and destroyed with brute force, pieces of the device lying on the floor mat. Beside them, tiny clumps of charred paper littered the floor.

The map, Mark thought, his heart pounding. *Someone got the map.*

His mind reeled. This was significant. Russel had never been completely honest with Mark about his past, and Mark had never pushed. He had never asked questions, because when you loved someone, you just had to be there for them—simple as that.

But now, Mark needed to understand what Russel had gotten him into.

And there was only one person who could help him untangle the web of lies that now threatened the life he had built:

Fleur.

CHAPTER TWENTY

IT WAS PAST MIDNIGHT, and Annie wasn't sleeping. Instead, she was curled in Ethan's arms, his snores making her increasingly aware of her own inability to leave the world behind. She stared at the ceiling, thinking about how close she was to finding answers about her brother's disappearance.

Russel was a good lead. And now, he was dead.

Annie's breath caught in her throat as she remembered the images of her brother's body that had been filed away in Police records. She had accessed them many years after he was murdered, hoping the act of looking up the past would give her closure.

It hadn't. Instead, it had driven home the cruelty of the world, and its capacity for pain.

Annie glanced up at Ethan, thinking about what she shared with him and what she didn't. She had let him into her world, but maybe that was a mistake. The safest position was to be alone. People could hurt you, and leave you, and the world didn't care how much you loved someone— so what was the point of loving at all? She wondered if maybe she'd be better off alone. Maybe people in general were better off alone.

Just then, there was a knock at the door. Annie sat upright, an involuntary gasp making her chest rattle. At the same moment, Ethan bolted awake, his snores a distant memory. He reached under his pillow and pulled out a loaded gun, pointing it at the door. With the other hand, he pushed Annie backwards, blocking her body with his own.

Annie blinked, shocked. "Do you keep that under your pillow *every* night?" She whispered in his ear.

"You're not the only one who's totally messed up, Annie," Ethan shook his head. Then, he yelled toward the door: "Who is it?"

"It's Cord!" A familiar voice from the other end of the door shouted. "There's a surprise gathering at the lake. You guys have to join."

Ethan visibly deflated, relief flooding his veins. Cord he could handle. He set down the gun, then stood, wearing nothing but flannel pajama pants. He pulled on a t-shirt and opened the door halfway, still cautious. Cord was standing on the other side, holding two paper lanterns in his hand.

"Thanks, Cord, but we're not really in a gathering mood."

"You *have* to come," Cord insisted, holding out the lanterns. "Tania planned it to help everyone with, you know, Russel—" Cord's voice caught in his throat.

"We're fine, really," Ethan insisted.

"But how else will you process it all?" Cord said, his eyes wide.

"Huh?" Ethan asked, rubbing his eyes. "Process it? Cord, I don't know— you just— bad things happen and you just deal with it however you can— "

"All on your own?"

There was a creaking sound as Annie stepped out of bed, wrapping a robe around her nightgown. She met Ethan at the door, standing beside him.

"It's just— " Cord continued, looking at Annie. "That's the

whole point of being here, isn't it? You don't have to deal with things on your own anymore. You have a village." He held out a lantern, offering it to Annie. "Just try. If you don't like it, you can leave."

Annie hesitated, feeling as if she were agreeing to something much larger than a gathering. But then, she reached out and took the unlit paper lantern, some small piece of her hoping Cord was right.

"We'll come," Annie said, nodding.

"Great!" Cord exclaimed, clapping his hands together after passing the other lantern to Ethan. "You know where the lake is?"

The pair nodded in response.

"See you in fifteen minutes. Dress warm. We'll wait for you."

CHAPTER TWENTY-ONE

THE FULL MOON hung heavy in the sky as Annie and Ethan crept down a winding path that led toward the forest. Round as a saucer, the moon's light cast a gentle glow over the tips of the trees, which bent under the heavy hand of a brisk, occasional wind.

Annie shuddered, putting her hands into the pockets of the sweatshirt she wore. She couldn't shake the feeling she was walking toward something she'd always needed but never known. She tried to brush away the strange, pressing emotion... after all, feelings weren't facts. But despite her best efforts, it persisted. "I'd like to take this moment to pitch a theory about our case," Ethan said, his voice breaking the silence.

Annie switched the lantern she was carrying into her other hand. "I'm always open," she said.

"Maybe they all killed Russel, and they're luring us into the woods because we're next."

"I'm ready to meet my fate, then, "Annie laughed. There was a long pause as Ethan took this in.

"You don't think that's... I mean, your current theory isn't that this is the creepy kind of commune and they all— "

"No." Annie reassured him. "My current theory is much sadder."

"Ah," Ethan said, and left it at that.

The thick blanket of trees began to thin as the pair followed the trail around a corner, suddenly finding themselves in a vast, open clearing.

Dew-drenched grass littered the valley, a soft carpet of green rolling down toward the center of the indentation, which was sandwiched between mountain ranges. Tiny flowers in shades of yellow and purple dotted the edge of the clearing, framed by the dense forest from which Annie and Ethan had just emerged. In the center of it all, a crystalline lake sat placid and smooth, its waters thinning as they reached toward the banks, following the moon on her path across the sky.

"Not a bad view," Ethan said, a low whistle escaping his lips as if the scene itself had knocked the air right out of him.

"Not bad at all," Annie answered, her voice a whisper that belonged in a church. She knew nothing she could say would capture the beauty.

The pair descended down the grassy knoll, approaching the group that awaited them by the water's edge. Tania stood at the head of the collective, holding an unlit lantern in her hand. Beside her was Guru Mett, dressed in a white robe. Next to him was Fleur, her hair in curls, the wind tussling her golden strands. Mark stood opposite Tania, Cord beside him — offering Annie and Ethan an over-eager wave— with a gruff-looking Banks on their flank.

Annie didn't miss Banks' sour expression— it was clear he hadn't wanted to be here, either. She wondered at his history, and what had brought him to the commune. She made a mental note to interview him at a later date. He had come to the commune too late to ever meet Russel. Still, he was a mystery, and mysteries needed solving.

"Welcome," Tania said, opening her arms wide. "Welcome

to the lantern ceremony." She motioned for Annie and Ethan to join her. They did, and the entire group stood elbow-to-elbow, the line of them looking out at the lake.

"To our new guests," Tania said, nodding at Annie, Ethan, and Banks, "we owe some explanation. You see, we've told you our rules but haven't explained why they are in place. And in a community built on equality, transparency is key." Tania's eyes turned glassy as she stared out at the water, the moonlight coloring her irises a careful shade of brown.

"The reason we don't discuss the past here in *Serenity Peaks* isn't just because we believe it's best to leave it all behind, or because our members sometimes come from difficult situations." Tania glanced at Fleur, who looked down at the ground. Annie took in the moment, and didn't miss the exchange. "The reason we don't discuss the past," Tania continued, "is that we believe society has the rules of life all wrong."

Ethan elbowed Annie, raising his eyebrows at her. *See,* his face seemed to say. "This is where it gets weird," he whispered. Annie stifled a laugh, and Tania looked at Ethan with a smirk that said she'd heard him.

"This isn't a cult-speech, don't worry," Tania shook her head at Ethan. "It's merely an explanation of why we do the things we do. We leave the past behind because we believe the way we lived in the outer world wasn't actually how humans were meant to exist. When humanity first formed, we lived in cooperative villages near family and friends, and we depended on each other for survival. Now, across America, we see an epidemic of loneliness. To support capitalism, people move into tiny apartments in big cities. They hardly know their neighbors. They're addicted to cell phones and technology, allowing social media sites and chat boards to take the place of real human interaction. And if you fail to survive in that brutal silo— if you struggle to stay afloat without community and a village— if you're one of the unlucky ones who is forgotten or left behind— you're medicated, abandoned, hospitalized, or overlooked." Tania pointed over the mountain range in the direction of the only road that led to town. "Out there, if you fail, society will allow you to meet your end." She looked to her left and right at the residents of *Serenity Peaks.* "But here, we won't allow any person in our tribe to sink. We are here for each other, from beginning to end. Sometimes we disagree. Isn't that right, Guru Mett?"

"I've mediated my fair share of disputes," he smiled. "Had one of my own last week with Mark about the boundaries of my garden—"

"Your vining plant is strangling my cucumber!" Mark exclaimed with such seriousness the entire group couldn't help but laugh.

"We have our disputes," Tania continued, "But we support each other. We keep each other safe. We remember that our natural state is to live in community. And as the world grows lonelier, we fight to maintain a lifestyle that's true to how human beings were meant to live. That said, we understand letting go of the past can be difficult." She held up her lantern for example. "And that's where the lantern ceremony comes in. We invite you to let go of something you'd like to leave behind. Something you don't want to carry as you continue on your journey at *Serenity Peaks.* Cord?"

Cord smiled and reached into his bag, pulling out a lighter and a pile of Sharpies. "Everyone take one," he said, moving through the group and offering each person a marker. "Write something on your lamp that you want to let go of. Together, we'll light the candles in the center of the lantern and let them go over the lake."

A hush settled on the group as everyone retreated to their individual tasks. Annie and Ethan sat in a pair, and Annie tried to scan the rest of the group for insights. Fleur hovered over her lantern, drawing some kind of picture that was difficult to make out in the dark. Tania and Guru Mett were shoulder- to-shoulder, writing on their lanterns with ease. Cord was trying to offer a lantern to Banks, who refused.

"Just try it," Cord said in a whisper, pushing the lantern toward Banks.

"No thanks," Banks said, shaking his head. "Not for me."

"You'll find it really freeing."

"Look, *kid*," Banks said, his tone on edge. "I fucking said I don't want—"

There was a tap on Banks' shoulder. He wheeled around, finding Fleur standing beside him. She stared at him for a moment in her quiet, strange way, then stood on her tiptoes and whispered something in his ear.

He took a step back as if she had hit him, his eyes wide like saucers. He ran his hand over his face, trying to process something that was too big for him in the moment.

"It's true," Fleur said to Banks. "And so can you. If you're brave enough."

Then, she left him, returning to her own lantern. Banks reeled, then— slowly, as if his hands weren't his own— he took a marker and a lantern from Cord, who slinked away. Banks hunched over the lantern, scrawling something on its surface in tiny letters that were impossible to make out.

Later, when the group was finished, Tania lined everyone up by the shore of the lake. Cord lit the candles within the lanterns, the flames flickering in the dark of the night sky. The group held their lanterns up, and at the same time, released them, a handful of regrets floating upward.

Annie watched as the lanterns careened toward the moon, gaining height with a boldness that said they thought they would fly forever, blissfully unaware that one day their candles would run out.

"What did you write on yours?" Annie said to Ethan, surprised to find that her voice was tight in her throat, and the words came out heavy.

"The FBI," he said, an edge to his tone. He took his hand in hers. "It's over for me. We'll have to build our own intelligence agency with people we trust." He smiled at her, noticing that her eyes were red. "What did you put, Annie?"

"My brother's name," she whispered. "I have to let it go. Whether I solve his murder or not. I have to let him go."

Beside them, Tania turned to the group, her back to the lake. "Thank you for your bravery," she said, smiling. "I don't care what you all wrote on your lanterns. I don't even care if you're successful in leaving the past behind. The only thing I want you to take from tonight, is the simple knowledge— " she paused, "— that you are not alone."

And— although she was there with a purpose, and for a job— Annie couldn't help but feel that, by coming to *Serenity Peaks*, she might have found something even better.

CHAPTER TWENTY-TWO

BANKS

WHEN BANKS MADE it back to his cabin after the lantern ceremony, he was relieved to finally be alone. He slammed the door to the bungalow with a heavy thud, his heart racing as he paced across the room.

His mind reeled, taking him back to the moment Fleur had whispered in his ear.

Banks had thought he was invisible. He was sure that no one here had seen him or caught on to what he was tasked with completing. And then— out of nowhere— this *girl* had laid bare the things he had tried in earnest to keep secret. She had looked not at him, but *through* him, without fear of death or retribution.

Banks sat on the bed, taking his head in his hands. It unnerved him, seeing this girl who was so willing to speak the unspeakable. Fleur's move had been a daring one. She had earmarked herself as a target. How could she look death in the face without the slightest hint of fear? Her bravery made Banks feel small. And he hated nothing more than feeling small.

If he had an ounce of her courage, he would have left by now. The only thing that kept him tied to his organization—

The Collective— was the knowledge that leaving would surely result in his death. They had more resources than him. More money. Once you were in, you were in for life.

And yet— this young woman had stared him in the face and feared for nothing. Shame rippled through Banks' body.

Just then, his cell phone buzzed. Banks removed it from the drawer of the bedside table, checking the message within.

It was from his employer. A picture of Annie and Ethan filled the screen. Simple directions were outlined underneath:

UNKNOWN

New orders— Eliminate.

Banks swallowed hard, wishing very suddenly that what Tania had said was true, and that a person really *could* leave the past behind.

But of course, it wasn't true. And now, the past had caught up with Annie and Ethan. Banks' mind whirred as he began to make a plan. He would need to make it look like an accident. Too much had happened already in this quaint, quiet commune.

He would need to hurry.

CHAPTER TWENTY-THREE

ANNIE AND ETHAN had only just shut the door to their cabin when Annie grabbed her sweater off a hook near the door and peeked out the window to check that the coast was clear. Then, she moved toward the front door and grabbed the handle, ready to strike out again.

"What are you doing?" Ethan exclaimed. He was happy to be inside, away from the cold night air and the memories the release of the lanterns had stirred within him. He already had one foot out of his pants when Annie reached for the door.

"I'm going to retrieve the lanterns, of course." Annie clocked Ethan's surprised expression. "To see what everyone wrote on them," she clarified. "They may not be allowed to talk about the past, here, but understanding the past could be key to finding out who killed Russel. And more importantly, I have some suspicions to confirm."

"But—" Ethan sputtered, motioning at the Keurig in the corner. "I was going to make a cup of tea and light the fireplace and—"

Annie stared at him as if nothing he was saying was in the least bit relevant.

Ethan sighed, realizing this was a fight he couldn't win.

He shook his head, putting one leg back inside his jeans with a resigned expression. He grabbed his own sweater and a pair of gloves for good measure. Then, he reached into his duffel bag and grabbed a Swiss army knife, followed by an FBI standard-issue flashlight he kept for emergencies. He clicked on the light before leaning over to kiss Annie. "It's a good thing I love you," he said.

Together, they made their way back into the thick, dark night, a scatterplot of stars twinkling overhead. The silence engulfed them as they headed back toward the lake, arriving quickly at the water's frosted edge. They stared out at the glassy lake, trying to calculate which direction the lanterns might have blown.

"We need to head North," Annie said, pointing across the water toward a cluster of trees in the distance. "When we released the lanterns, the wind was blowing that way. The candles were so small— tea candles. The burn down would've been quick. I doubt those lanterns stayed airborne for more than ten or fifteen minutes."

"Roger that," Ethan agreed. He followed her around the circumference of the lake, which thankfully was a small body of water and not a vast ocean to be overcome. After a brief hike they reached the cluster of trees, and pushed their way into the dense foliage, pine needles crackling under their boots.

"Make sure to look up," Annie said thoughtfully. "The trees grow close enough together it's likely the lanterns would have landed in the branches."

Ethan did as she said and they scouted both the ground at their feet and the branches overhead, Ethan's flashlight like a beacon in the night, highlighting an otherwise unseeable forest of black.

"Wait," Annie said, stopping as she spotted something on the ground. Ethan pointed his light in the direction of her concern and Annie bent down, discovering the tattered remains of a paper lantern. A few shreds of beige were gathered on the ground, the edges singed and destroyed.

"We found one but it's no good," Annie said, turning the paper over to look for writing, but finding none. "Either there was nothing written on it to begin with, or the side with writing was destroyed."

"Tells us we're in the right area, though," Ethan said.

They resumed their search, feeling encouraged by their recent discovery. Even though the find wasn't fruitful, it told Annie that they were on the right track. Then, she spotted it— a ripped, paper lantern caught high in the branches of a tree, dangling from the edge of a branch like a bat in a cave.

"Can you reach it?" she asked Ethan, who stared at her, aghast.

"That's— " He looked up, trying to calculate the distance. "Probably twenty feet up!"

"But you're six feet tall so it's really only like fourteen feet up," Annie said encouragingly.

Ethan couldn't deny her point, so he passed her his flashlight and cracked his knuckles before reaching toward the ground in a deep stretch. He sank into a runner's lunge, first on one side and then the other. Annie watched him patiently. "That's great," she said, nodding. "Stretching is important."

Having sufficiently postponed the inevitable, Ethan stepped toward the tree and found a foothold in a low branch. He pushed himself upward, and in no time at all was ascending the twisted branches. "How's it going?" Annie called up to him.

"Just like when I was a kid!" Ethan shouted down to her, not wanting to seem weak in the face of danger. For a moment, his hand slipped, and he almost missed a branch. His life flashed before his eyes - a tangled web of choices, some good and some bad, including this one- before he managed to secure a grip on a lower, weaker brand. He wiped his brow and took a breath before continuing the ascent, this time with even greater care.

Finally, he reached the lantern. He stretched his arm out long and pulled it from the branches, careful not to damage it further in the process. His descent down the tree was quick and nimble, and by the time he landed on the ground, he was thoroughly exhausted.

"That was amazing!" Annie said, removing the lantern from his hands. Ethan lay on his back on the forest floor, exhaling so heavily his breath turned to steam in the chill of the night air. "Thanks, "he said proudly. "I've been trying not to skip arm day at the gym."

"I meant our luck!" Annie answered, holding up the lantern. "It's in great shape. Barely ripped at all." Despite herself, Annie noticed Ethan's disappointed expression. She knelt beside him, putting a hand on his chest. "But you," she said, "You were amazing before you climbed the tree, and you're still amazing after." She kissed him with a deep, private longing, and Ethan felt that he was right where he belonged. Annie had that effect on him. Whether he was in an ocean- side town, or at a commune in the mountains, Annie made him feel at home. "Do you know who it belongs to?" Ethan asked, sitting up to brush the dirt off his pants.

"In fact, I do," Annie smiled. "Each lantern was a different color. Fleur's was pink. Mine was pastel blue. This one is green."

"Who does it belong to?" Ethan asked.

"Banks," Annie smiled. "A very lucky development, considering he's a mystery I've been wanting to solve."

Ethan stood, looking over Annie's shoulder to get a better look at the lantern. "What's it say? What does the mysterious Mr. Banks want to leave behind?"

Amie flipped the lantern over, showing Ethan two simple words written in uneven scrawl.

"The Collective," she read aloud. "Any idea what it means?"

"Only a suspicion. "Annie said. She held the lantern with care as she turned and started the long walk back toward the Commune. She lost herself in thought as they emerged from the dense cluster of trees, rounding the edge of the lake that led back toward the valley.

Suddenly, Ethan's arm grabbed the back of her sweater, stopping her in her tracks. Wordlessly, he brought a finger to his lips. Annie took the cue and froze, listening. The sound of voices echoed in the distance, carrying over the treetops. Someone else was walking in the forest at night, signaling to Annie and Ethan:

They were not alone.

Ethan clicked off his flashlight, plunging them into darkness. Together, Annie and Ethan crouched low and advanced toward the intruders, careful to stay concealed under the blanket of night.

CHAPTER TWENTY-FOUR

MARK

OUT IN THE FOREST, Mark shivered against the cold. He stared up at a towering pine tree, trying to think of something to say. In front of him stood Fleur, her arms crossed, a question in her eyes.

Since Mark had moved to *Serenity Peaks*, he'd learned to see the forest differently— to understand it as a well-meaning friend instead of a vast, empty wilderness filled with trials. Still, in moments like this, the forest somehow managed to find a way to be imposing. Even though Mark was an environmentalist, nature had always terrified him. Something about her raw power made him feel small. But unlike most men, Mark's awe in the face of natural forces made him want to protect the Earth— not dominate it.

Mark let his gaze fall back to Fleur, and he gave her the only answer he could muster:

"... I understand you want me to do what Russel asked, but it's too much." Mark's voice rasped low, his breath visible in the cold night air. He and Fleur stood amidst the towering pines of *Serenity Peaks*, their figures shrouded by darkness. "I've done favor after favor for Russel, but I have to draw the line somewhere. He gave me no explanation as to why—"

"Because he *couldn't!*" Fleur exclaimed, stomping her foot on the cold, wet Earth. "It would only put you in greater danger—"

"See, that's the thing," Russel shook his head. "I don't know how much danger I'm in. I don't know what I'm fighting *for*. I'm just supposed to take one man's word—"

"He trusted you," Fleur whispered fiercely, her golden hair a muted halo in the moonlight. "He didn't leave this plan for just anyone. He left it to you. And he left it to me."

Mark shifted in discomfort, his wethered hands balled into fists. "I found a map in my car." He paused, trying to read Fleur's reaction. She raised a single eyebrow. It was a subtle confirmation, but enough to reveal that she had expected as much. "You knew, then? You knew it was there?"

"He didn't tell me the whole plan," Fleur allowed, her voice measured. "He didn't tell *anyone* the whole plan—"

"But you knew about the map."

"I knew he left something for you in the truck," Fleur confirmed. "I think he told me because he was worried you wouldn't go through with it, and it turns out he was right."

"Well it doesn't matter anymore because the map was destroyed," Mark said. Fleur gasped, putting a hand to her mouth. "That's right," Mark nodded. "So you see now, the danger here? Whatever he was running from, it's here now, in *Serenity Peaks*. I could be sending these people into a mess if I do what Russel asked and give them the car, plus the map—" His tone edged with frustration as he struggled to articulate the weight of his discovery. "If I'd known—"

"Known what?" Her words cut through his hesitation like a knife. "That he'd involve us in something this big? You wouldn't have agreed?"

Mark exhaled. Trying to make Fleur see the situation through the eyes of an adult instead of those of a child was difficult. "Fleur, what Russel asked— it's not fair— not to us or to Annie and Ethan. They're good detectives. Most likely good people. They don't deserve to be tangled up in... in whatever this is without so much as an explanation."

"Fairness lost sight of me a long time ago. And when he died, I realized it never existed," Fleur countered, stepping closer. Her eyes, usually pools of calm, were lit with fire. "We *owe* him this much."

Mark stepped back from her, shaking his head. "But at what cost, Fleur? At what cost?"

"Fair is keeping a promise," Fleur insisted, her voice barely a whisper. The forest around them seemed to hold its breath. Her eyes glistened in the sparse moonlight, silver tracks of unshed tears threatening to break free.

Mark's gaze lingered on her face, delicate sorrow etched into her features. She looked so childlike. So young. He remembered when he'd been that way. Youthful passion. Naive trust— it was what had led him to try and protect the environment through the wrong means. "Russel isn't here to argue this," Mark replied, his own voice strained with the weight of unspoken words. "So you and I have to make the best decision we can right now, tonight. But we don't have to agree. We can each do what we think is right."

"No, we don't," a tear breached Fleur's defenses, trailing down her cheek. "We don't have to agree. But I can tell you— I made him a promise, too. I've been waiting for the right moment and..." She took a deep breath, steadying herself against the turmoil within. "It's time. The detectives need to know everything. I'm going to *tell* them everything."

The revelation hung heavy between them, a tangible presence in the night air. Mark's mind reeled, images of Russel—tough yet tender, aged beyond his years—flashed before him.

"If that's what Russel wanted you to do, then do it," Mark said, nodding. "I have to believe he wouldn't have asked you to put yourself in danger. You meant so much to him. And he meant the world to me."

"He meant more to you than a friend," Fleur observed, her gaze meeting his squarely now. "He would never say—"

Mark hesitated, a flicker of vulnerability crossing his rugged features. Silence stretched, taut as a bowstring, before he nodded, conceding the truth. "Yes. Russel meant more to me than a friend." His voice broke as he acknowledged the truth.

A soft sigh escaped Fleur, and she stepped closer, her presence a balm to his unquiet heart. "I'm glad you told me," she murmured, and despite the chill, warmth bloomed between them. "Grieving alone... it's unbearable. Dad would never say if it was more than friends. I'm not sure why."

"I think he felt as if he'd put you through enough," Mark answered, remembering the long conversations he'd shared with Russel late at night in front of a roaring fireplace. Russel had told him that Fleur was his daughter, and sworn him to secrecy.

"What did he tell you about where we came from?"

"Very little," Mark answered. "Just that it was bad. And dangerous. And bigger than I could possibly understand. It took him months to trust me enough to tell me you were his daughter. I think he only did it because he wanted someone to look after you in case something happened to him."

Fleur stood still under the moonlight, wanting to believe what Mark had said. The wind whipped around the pines, and Fleur thought about the nature of family— what it meant to create one from disparate people with no genetic connection. She wondered if being connected by love was just as powerful as being connected by genetics.

"I'm alone now," Fleur gulped, afraid.

"No, you're not," Mark said, stepping toward her. "That's the meaning of *Serenity Peaks*. You are part of a community. You are not alone."

"I *feel* alone is what I meant to say," Fleur answered. "I wish everyone knew. They'd understand if they knew our ties to him were different than theirs— They'd be here for us. I hate this rule. That we don't talk about the past."

Mark's movements were deliberate as he closed the distance that grief had carved between them. He wrapped his arms around Fleur, a gesture that spoke volumes in the silence of the forest. His hands were steady and sure, a contrast to the tremble in his voice as he pulled her close, just as her father used to.

"You're not alone," he whispered against her hair, the strands catching on his stubble.

Fleur's body relaxed into the embrace, her breath hitching softly. "How can you be so sure?" she asked him.

Mark pulled back just enough to look at her, his eyes intent on her face, hands planted firmly on her shoulders as if he were tethering her to the Earth. "Because I promised your Dad that if something happened to him, I'd take care of you," he said, each word punctuated with a weight that seemed to anchor them both to the spot. "And *that* is a promise I will always keep."

Fleur burst into tears and leaned once again into Mark's shoulder. He did his best to calm her underneath the moonlight, thinking about how he could never— under any circumstances— allow harm to come to the frail, charming offspring of the man he had once loved so deeply.

Mark was attentive— so concerned, so *focused*— on Fleur, that he didn't spot the two human shapes backing away from behind a shrub, their forms barely visible in the darkness. It was the detectives— Annie and Ethan— making their way back to camp, after having heard absolutely everything.

CHAPTER TWENTY-FIVE

FLEUR

THE CABIN'S TIMBERS GROANED. Fleur sat on the bed and took off her boots, looking at the mud that was caked onto their grooved bottoms. Her conversation with Mark had left her rattled. There was so much grief to unpack. So much that lay ahead.

Fleur had barely settled onto her old, creaking mattress when the knock came—sharp, unexpected. She stiffened, her heart quickening.

"Mark?" Her voice was a whisper lost in the vastness of the night.

"It's Annie," came a soft voice from the other side of the door. "And Ethan. I know it's late. I hope you'll open the door anyway."

Fleur rose from the bed, trance-like. She crossed the room, her fingers grazing the cool metal of the doorknob before swinging it open. Annie and Ethan stood on her cabin's small porch, their features etched with purpose.

"I knew you'd come back. But now?" Fleur said.

"We heard you in the woods," Annie said honestly. "Talking to Mark."

"You were following me?"

"We were looking for lanterns," Ethan offered, holding up the one he'd retrieved earlier. "You just happened to be there."

"A lucky accident," Fleur said skeptically.

"Russel was your father," Annie said, offering a statement instead of a question. "I need to know what you know about the Coll—"

"Shh!" Fleur's hand shot up, slicing through Annie's words. Her eyes widened in fear. She dared a glance around the perimeter. "Don't say it. Not here."

"Of course," Annie agreed, although— she wasn't afraid. She didn't care if the Collective knew who she was. All Annie wanted was the truth.

"It's safer inside," Fleur stepped aside, gesturing them into the warmth of her home.

The door shut behind them with a decisive click, sealing out the night. In the stillness of the small cabin, Annie and Ethan took two vacant seats at a worn coffee table. Fleur sat on the bed across from them, reaching underneath and pulling out her sketchbook. Her fingers trembled as they traced its edges, running over pages filled with the ink stains that had defined her life so far. She settled cross-legged on the bed as she flipped it open. Annie and Ethan perched on the edge of mismatched chairs, rigid.

"You said he put my name on the Pictionary game for you to find?" Fleur asked. Annie and Ethan nodded in agreement. "It's because he wanted me to use my drawings to tell you the truth. Everything began here," Fleur murmured, her soft-spoken voice carrying a weight that seemed to fill the small cabin. She turned the sketchbook towards them, revealing a drawing of a young man with eyes full of hope. A hood covered his face, his chin covered in scruff.

"Russel," she said, with a reverence reserved for saints and sinners alike. "My Dad. The way he tells it, he was lost back then. Brilliant. But one mistake branded him. He had an education from a top school, but a felony drug charge kept him from doing anything meaningful with it. Then he found *them*, and they gave him meaning. They welcomed him into their group. Even got him a cover job at the CIA. They made him feel like he belonged."

Annie leaned in, her sharp eyes absorbing every line, every shade that composed the image of Russel. "The Collective gave him purpose."

"Exactly." Fleur nodded, her gaze falling to the next page as she turned it. "A place for his talents, when society told him he had nothing to offer."

Ethan's jaw clenched, the muscles in his neck taut. "They prey on vulnerable people."

"Always," Fleur confirmed, her voice barely above a whisper.

The sketchbook rustled softly as another page turned. Fleur paused at a sketch of a baby cradled in a woman's arms. Her own innocent, unknowing face stared back at them from the paper, captured in shades of charcoal.

"Me," she said, her finger hovering over the infant's sketched outline. "And my mother. She had problems that kept her from being around for me. She didn't tell my dad she was pregnant with me either. He only ran around with her because he was trying to fit in. It makes more sense now than it ever did," Fleur said, thinking about Mark, and what he had revealed to her about the nature of his relationship with Russel. "So, neither of my parents could do much with me. And I ended up just being raised by different people in the group."

"Raised by the Collective..." Ethan's voice trailed off, the implications hanging heavy in the air.

"Passing from one member to another. Never belonging to anyone but always observing." Fleur's eyes held a distant glint, as though peering into a past that refused to stay buried. "The bad part was they weren't all nice. *Most* of them weren't. The good part is that I learned about how they do things. I know more than the average member because I saw so many different people in the group attending to their business."

"Your dad— when did he find out he had a child?" Annie asked.

"Not until much later." Fleur turned the page, revealing a stark sketch: a teenage girl, drenched by relentless rain, standing beside a man. The alley they occupied was dark, save for the diffuse glow of a flickering streetlight. "I was fifteen," she whispered, tracing the outline of the sketched figures. "That's when he found me."

Annie leaned forward, her gaze fixed on the drawing. "Russel?"

"For me, finding Russel— my Dad— changed everything." Fleur's fingers paused over the teenager's drawn face. "He helped me escape."

"Out of the Collective?" Ethan asked, his voice low and urgent.

"He'd been having doubts for a long time. He'd been thinking of leaving himself, but not before he could find something that would ruin them once and for all. And then — when he learned about me— he wanted to get us both out."

"Where did you go?"

"*Serenity Peaks*," Fleur's lips curved into a smile as she motioned around the room. "A new start. Dad thought I would do well in a commune because I was raised by a group. He worried I wouldn't know how to function in the outside world, and he thought *Serenity Peaks* would be a safe place. He took a lot of time interviewing Tania and learning about it in secret. But we couldn't let everyone know we were related. He said the Collective would be looking for a father and daughter on the run. So, we became strangers to each other in the eyes of the group."

"Protection through anonymity." Annie nodded, understanding flashing in her sharp eyes.

"Exactly." Fleur's voice was a hushed confession. "We arrived separately. Dad wired the money from two different accounts. I got here first, and he showed up a few days later. As far as I know, nobody here has ever figured it out. It might seem extreme, but the thing you have to understand is that The Collective isn't just thugs and thieves. It's a network. They're everywhere, and they're powerful."

"Government?" Annie asked, her tone slicing through the charged air.

"Among others. You can't imagine the reach they have. They were able to get Dad a job with the CIA because another member worked there. That connection got him in, which only let them deepen their reach. That's how they do it. Person by person, they burrow into our most important organizations like ticks." Fleur blinked, and the blue-green depths of her irises shimmered with an intensity that seemed to argue with her delicate face. "Drugs, humans, secrets—they traffic in them all."

Annie's hand clenched into a fist, signaling her rising anger—or determination. "We'll find them."

"They're closer than you think," Fleur offered. "What they did to my Dad proves as much—" her voice caught in her throat as she choked back tears. "They came for him, and they'll get me next. I don't even care. If they take me, that's fine. I'm so tired of running. Maybe tired of even being in the world," Fleur let the words fall from her lips like poison. She'd been thinking it long enough. Saying it didn't feel much worse.

Annie reached across the divide and put a hand on Fleur's knee. "I know how this feels," Annie whispered. "But your dad would want you to fight. To live."

"You don't know anything," Fleur shirked away from her touch.

"Someone killed my brother," Annie said softly. "He was about to buy his first home. And Ethan's sister was helping him. It was her first job as a real estate agent. She's been missing over a decade. They were murdered by a repeat offender. A killer the press called the Real Estate Ripper. And, apparently, he has ties to the Collective."

"And if our last source got it right," Ethan said, his voice low, "… to your father. That's why we're here. Our evidence pointed to Russel Grey being the Real Estate Ripper."

"Impossible," Fleur whispered, the denial quick and fierce. "My father wasn't a killer." Her eyes flicked between them, defiant. "But it's possible that he—"

"What?" Ethan asked.

"It's possible he worked with the Real Estate Ripper."

"Explain," Annie demanded, her posture rigid with urgency.

"Violent people? They find a home in the Collective," Fleur started, moving back to her sketchbook. Her hand trembled slightly as she turned the pages, revealing a sketch of a group of shadowed figures standing in front of a home. "Your Real Estate Ripper is probably one of them. When I moved between different members of the group as a kid, sometimes they were staying in vacant houses that were listed for sale. They used these homes for everything. Mailing addresses for fraudulent documents, safe houses, human trafficking. The owners didn't know, or if they did, they were threatened into silence."

"Maybe our guy sees it as a game," Ethan muttered, rubbing the bridge of his nose as if to fend off a headache or worse— the truth. He looked at Annie, pain in his eyes. "He works with the Collective as his day job at these safe houses, then kills opportunistically when the chance comes along."

"Understand," Fleur said, locking eyes with Annie, "the Collective attracts the most psychopathic, terrible people in the world. The group actively seeks them out."

"It's possible he used their resources to locate victims," Ethan agreed, nodding. "But he was killing for his own—"

"Gratification?" Annie swallowed hard. The profile they were beginning to build lined up. And it certainly didn't match Russel Grey.

"My Dad was determined to dismantle the Collective in any way he could. To atone." Fleur's gaze flicked to Annie's, searching, questioning. "Before he died, he told me that you'd come. He said I should trust you." She swallowed hard, a tear slipping down her cheek. "But how can I trust anyone?"

Annie's reply was swift, cutting through the tension. "We can finish what he started. We can do it together."

"My Dad had a plan," Fleur said, closing the sketchbook and clutching it tight to her chest. "But he never shared it all. Just pieces, to a few trusted people." She met Annie's eyes again, more tears tracking down her face. "This is my piece— he asked me to tell you what I know about the Collective. To be honest with you. To trust. He said... one day, if I did that, it would all make sense."

Annie leaned in. "Fleur. Russel left us the pieces of a puzzle to solve. I think— I think your dad knew someone was onto him. And he didn't want anyone but Ethan and me to put it all together. He assigned each member of the Commune to a board game as a clue."

"That's why I was Pictionary," Fleur said, understanding. "And Mark. Did his game have something to do with a car?"

"Hot Wheels," Annie smiled.

Despite herself, Fleur couldn't help but grin. "I knew he was asking Mark about the truck," she clucked her tongue. "But the games... of *course* he would hide everything behind the games."

Annie sighed, her voice suddenly heavy. "Fleur, I promise you... we're going to get to the bottom of this. You have my word."

Fleur hesitated, searching Annie's face for something she

could believe in. If she found it, she didn't say. Instead, she offered a quick, curt nod. "Thank you," she whispered, her voice steadier now. She reached into her sketch book, flipping through the pages before pausing at a single sketch. A ripping sound echoed across the cabin as she tore it from the book without fear. She passed it to Annie, who scanned the image there:

A man—Russel— sitting in front of a board game, laughing.

"You can have that," Fleur said.

"We couldn't—" Ethan started to say, before Fleur cut him off.

"Take it," Fleur insisted. "I want you to remember who made all this possible when you take them down. The Collective, I mean."

"Well, our focus is finding the Real Estate Ripper," Ethan cautioned, holding a hand in the air. "I don't know if we're prepared to—"

"We'll take it," Annie said solemnly. "And we won't let you down. That's a promise."

As the detectives turned to leave, Fleur felt less alone than she had in days. She shut the door softly behind them, thinking about where she had come from, and what lay ahead. She glanced at the drawings that lined her cabin walls. So many of them featured Russel. Fleur collapsed onto her bed, hoping— praying— that her dad had known what he was doing when he decided to trust these two Detectives.

CHAPTER TWENTY-SIX

MARK

IT WAS the middle of the night, and Mark was dreaming. It was the kind of nightmare that made a man relive his life in a loop. In the dream, he was leaning against a tall building, a white envelope in his hand. He knew— without seeing it— that the envelope contained devastation in the form of white powder. A chemical nerve agent. All he had to do was deliver it to the business that lived in the glossy, horrific skyscraper he was currently leaning up against, and the deed would be done. But in the dream, his legs wouldn't move. They were glued to the sidewalk, stuck in place. He realized at that moment his only choice was to use the powder on himself.

A knock shattered the night's silence. Mark's eyes snapped open, heart hammering against his ribs like a trapped bird. Did the knock come from his dream?

A second series of urgent knocks emanated from the front door, making it clear Mark was back in the real world. He rolled out of bed, the cold of the wooden floorboards seeping through his socks. The knock came again, urgent. Fear coiled in his gut. No one this eager to see him ever wanted anything but trouble.

He shuffled to the kitchenette, grabbing a knife from a

butcher's block on the counter's edge. The blade's familiar weight a small comfort. As he gripped the knife, another knock echoed, more insistent. Mark approached the door, each step heavy with dread.

"Who's there?" His voice was gravel, rough from sleep.

"Detective Annie Hudson and Agent Ethan Beckett."

What a couple of assholes, coming by so late. Still, Mark slid the knife into his front sweatpants pocket and opened the door. The porch light threw long shadows behind Annie and Ethan, their faces etched with purpose.

"Mark." Annie's gaze flicked to the knife in his pocket, then back to his eyes. "Why the hardware?"

"Late visitors bring trouble," Mark said. "What do you want?"

"Russel's truck," Annie replied, her words cutting through the chill air.

Mark took in the request, his face falling. His conversation with Fleur earlier in the evening looped through his mind. He thought about her wide eyes, the shocked sadness that he wouldn't obey Russel's requests word-for-word. And the truck. The truck that was never truly his.

Mark's sigh was a white cloud dissipating into the night. He nodded once, resigned. "Let's go see the truck."

They trekked through the commune's sleeping heart, moonlight casting silver trails across the grounds. Annie and Ethan fell into step behind Mark, who led the way with a slumped stance that said he was walking to his own execution.

He stopped by a hulking shape, its silhouette distinct under the stars. "Here she is," he murmured, patting the truck's side. Its once-drab chassis now gleamed with a sheen of white, eco-friendly paint, the engine modified to sip corn oil like fine wine.

"Russel's gift," Mark said, his voice low. He unlocked the

door, the creak breaking the nocturnal chorus. "And my rebirth."

Annie's eyes narrowed. "Rebirth?"

"Jail changes you," he admitted. A hand ran over the recycled dash. "Russel and I had both done some time, albeit for different reasons. In my youth, I was an environmental activist who thought the only way to teach polluting companies a lesson was violent action. Anthrax," he said, answering the question in Annie's eyes. "I delivered it to an Oil & Gas company. No one was hurt," he said quickly. "They detected it before it could—you know." He looked down in shame. "Once I got out, I just needed to start again. We both wanted clean slates, Russel and me. He brought the truck with him, and it became a shared project. I cleaned it up. We both used it to go into town. Russel took the old girl on some longer adventures…"

"Where'd he go with it?" Ethan's question hung between them, heavy.

"God knows. Weeks at a time, gone." Mark shrugged, a ghost of frustration in his eyes. "He wouldn't say where. That's the thing about this place. You learn to leave people alone as they sort out a past they can't even talk about."

The silence grew taut until Mark broke it again. "Russel said you'd come. 'Give the Detectives the truck,' he told me." Mark met Annie's gaze, a flicker of something unreadable in his own. "Like he predicted his ending. It's almost as if he knew someone was going to get him. Like he knew he was going to die."

"This wasn't the first time he'd asked you for a favor?" Annie asked, sensing something deeper in Mark's resigned expression.

"No," Mark said, shaking his head. "He asked me for a lotta favors over the years. And one of them involved *you.*" He paused, making room for their shocked expressions. "Russel knew about a case in Watersborough, Massachusetts.

A man named Mr. Markin was killed and a letter was sent to the FBI."

"We solved that case," Ethan answered. "Annie did."

"It was you who hired me," Annie realized, eyes wide. "You're the one who sent me the letter asking me to investigate."

Mark nodded. "Russel said you needed to be involved because it was your chance to solve your own past. He'd been waiting for the perfect opportunity, monitoring crimes across the country. He said this one was what he'd been waiting for, and that you *had* to be hired. So, I was the one who made sure you were hired. He watched you, Annie. Believed in you."

"And the truck?" Annie pressed. "Why did Russel want us to have it?"

"He wouldn't say." Mark answered. "But I opened up the dashboard and I found a map inside, with a location circled out in the desert." Annie began to ask to see it, but Mark held up a hand. "It's gone. Someone destroyed it. It wasn't me. Someone broke into the truck and lit the damn thing on fire."

Annie began to pace, her footsteps light on the dusty earth beneath her feet. "The map. Russel wanted us to *go* somewhere—"

"His compound out in the desert," Mark sighed. "He never let me know the exact spot, but there's a town nearby he left me in once. Rachel, Nevada. Soon as I saw it on the map, I knew that was where he was sending you."

"We'll go right away," Ethan nodded. "This is what we've been hoping for—"

"Now, hold on," Mark advised, shaking his head. "Russel sent a lotta people in circles. I loved the man, but he was secretive. You better know what you're getting into—"

"We want it," Ethan said, ignoring Mark's warning. "The map. Can you recreate it?"

Russel considered. He remembered the area outline on the

page. It was a place he'd been before. "Not perfectly," he admitted. "But I could get you close."

"Fleur can help you," Annie suggested. "She'll draw what you describe."

Mark leaned against the truck, afraid the Detectives didn't understand the depth of the waters ahead. "You sure you want this?"

Annie nodded.

"Wherever Russel came from— what little he told me— it's a dark place. Not something anyone should be tangled up in."

"Then don't you get tangled up in it," Ethan offered. "*We* will."

"They took our siblings," Annie told him. "I need to see this to the end."

"The end?" Mark asked. "And where is that? Where does this lead?"

"It's safer not knowing," Annie's reply came swift, clipped. "That's why Russel never told you the entire story. It was his way of protecting you. Trust me," she stepped forward, putting a hand on his arm. "All the evidence points to the fact that Russel was trying to keep you safe. To keep you out of the mess he'd come from. You're stepping forward without knowing everything, but maybe you can make the leap of faith anyway."

Mark sighed. Leaps of faith had never worked out well for him in the past. It was a leap of faith that had led him to the outside of a skyscraper, holding an envelope of Anthrax. But here he was again, taking a leap. He was tender-hearted and had loved Russel. And— at the end of the day— that was all he could say for himself. Mark reached into his pocket and removed the keys to the truck. He passed them to Annie.

"These belong to you," he said, a pained look in his eye. "If you'll let me, I'd like to double-check the fuel system before I give her to you. You'll be hard-pressed to find a mechanic who can fix it out there."

"We would appreciate that," Annie agreed. "Thank you. We're not quite ready to leave yet anyway. Still solving a murder and whatnot."

"I'll give you the keys when you're ready to leave," Mark agreed."When you go, keep her under 75. Gets dicey the faster you go."

"I'll bring her back to you, if we make it out of all of this," Annie promised.

"Don't know why he'd ask me to let go of the truck— the last thing we worked on together. It's the last piece of him I got," Mark said, his voice tightening as a knot rose up in his throat.

"Of course it isn't," Annie said, shaking her head as if the answer were obvious: "Fleur is the last piece of him," she said. "And she needs you."

Mark nodded. "Fleur." And they left it at that. Silence fell, a tense agreement between the three of them, promises whispered under a blanket of crisp, night air.

CHAPTER TWENTY-SEVEN

WHEN MORNING CAME, the day felt lighter. Easier. Ethan stirred from the depths of his dreams. He blinked against the slanting rays of morning light that had evaded the curtains, and there she was—Annie, perched like some watchful raptor at the window, a steaming mug cradled in her hands.

"Morning," he rasped, voice thick with sleep.

"Morning," Annie replied, not turning away from the view of *Serenity Peaks*. Outside the window, the mountains stood like sculptures, their snow-covered peaks piercing the open sky. The landscape was beautiful. But— for Annie— an underlying tension clung to the air. And there was nothing she loved more than a little tension. A smile played on her lips.

"Are you smiling?" Ethan swung his legs over the edge of the bed, flexing stiff muscles.

"We're close." She glanced at him, a little pleased with herself. "The case is coming together. Just a couple of final pieces that need to fall into place."

"Who are we talking to today?"

"I like a yoga class as much as the next person," Annie offered.

"Guru Mett it is," Ethan agreed. His nod was slow but decisive. They were threading the needle, and the eye was almost in sight.

———

Guru Mett's yoga studio smelled of sandalwood and lemon oil. The wooden floors gleamed underfoot, reflecting the soft glow of morning as it filtered through diaphanous curtains. Guru Mett, a figure of quietude amidst the expanse of cushions and mats, rose to greet them. His smile was strained.

"Detective Hudson. Agent Beckett. Are you here for a private session or—"

"Guru Mett." Annie's greeting cut through the pleasantries. "We need to talk. About Russel."

Guru Mett stilled, the smile faltering but not quite vanishing. "I see," he said. He let the words sit, almost as if he was afraid saying anything else would only complicate his situation. Annie stepped forward, her footsteps echoing in the vacant studio.

"Russel left instructions," Annie pressed on, relentless. "For all of you. Everyone had a role to complete. But you haven't played yours. Is that correct?"

"I don't—"

"Russel left the game of Monopoly with your name on it," Annie continued. "So, I can only assume your task involved money. It's strange, though," Annie said, pacing a straight line. "I've been asking myself... why would Russel give the spiritual leader a task involving money? Unless he knew something about your past. Something that would make you the obvious choice."

Guru Mett folded his hands, nodding slowly in a kind of

resigned acceptance. "Money is the root of all evil," he murmured, almost to himself.

"Let's not dance around it," Ethan said, his tone firm but not unkind. "What did he ask you to do? Out with it. The truth."

Annie glanced at her partner, surprised at the subtle outburst. The personal nature of this case seemed to be getting to him, and for the first time, Annie realized that Ethan, too, was struggling. Here she had thought only days earlier that Ethan would be better off without her. Now— seeing him lose his ordinarily composed demeanor for even a moment— Annie realized that Ethan needed her, too.

The guru met their gaze, weighty silence enveloping the room before he spoke again, each word deliberate and measured.

"Truth is rarely pure and almost never simple," he began, almost cryptically, then paused when he noticed Ethan's agitated expression. A long exhale. "Fine," he offered, shaking off his Guru-esque performance. "You want the truth? Here it is."

Annie leaned in, her eyes never leaving Guru Mett's face.

"Start from the beginning," she said.

The guru's gaze dropped to his clasped hands. "In another life," he began, "I was a man of numbers, not of spirit." He lifted his eyes, a storm brewing in their depths. "A financial advisor."

Annie nodded, patient. "Go on."

"Confidence was my trade. Trust, my currency. But markets are unpredictable. I sought to outsmart them. The thing you have to understand is I never *meant* to hurt anybody. I was doing it all from a place of good. I just wanted to win. Became obsessed with it."

"And?" Ethan prompted, his jaw tightening.

"I failed," Mett swallowed, his Adam's apple bobbing. "I took my client's money and made some big bets that turned out to be wrong. So, to cover the losses, I shuffled funds. If I lost one investor's money, I just took from the next investor to show an increased balance in the first person's account."

"You stole," Ethan clarified.

Guru Mett shrugged as if the specifics weren't worth getting into. "It wasn't my intention but it was what happened. I'm a people pleaser at heart. I just wanted everyone to win. To see their accounts grow. But I bet the wrong way."

"You're a white-collar criminal," Annie said.

"Yes," Guru Mett agreed. "And I lost everything because of it. My houses were liquidated. Cars sold. I did my time, paid my dues, and with my last remaining pennies, came here. To *Serenity Peaks*. This place gave me the chance to start over. I brought my laptop, my past life's tether. I planned to bury it, along with my sins. Maybe do a ritual sacrifice. Light the thing on fire if I had to. I was settling into a spiritual path but then Tania—" Guru Mett paused, remembering.

"Tania intervened?" Annie asked.

"She asked me to manage the Commune's funds. Running this place is a lot for her. I think she figured trusting the spiritual guy with the money made sense."

"Did you ...?" Ethan asked. An accusation hung between the detectives and the man they sought to understand.

"Did I what, Agent Beckett?"

"Fall back into old habits?"

Guru Mett stood, his frame casting a long shadow across the bamboo floor. "Tania believed in redemption. In the power of this place to heal." His hand hovered above his heart. "And so, I believed. I can proudly say to you, I have *not* misappropriated commune funds. Ninety percent are in traditional ETFs. Safe and sound."

"And the other ten percent?" Annie asked.

"The other ten percent I placed into crypto," Guru Mett smiled. He couldn't help but beam at the results of his latest financial experiment. "I mean, you couldn't expect me not to bet at *all*. People have to have a little fun in life."

"And?"

"And this time— I bet *right*." The Guru's cheeks flushed, thrilled at himself. "The money I put in crypto for the commune as multiplied in value tenfold. This place is rich. And I've kept it all in the commune's name. I love this place. And I intend to do right by it. I believe this opportunity was presented to me as a chance to atone—"

"Belief is good," Ethan said, stepping closer. "Proof is better."

"Proof," the guru echoed, his voice barely louder than a sigh.

"Show us," Annie demanded.

With a nod, Guru Mett leaned down to a loose floorboard and pried it open. He pulled out a laptop, setting it on a small desk covered in tapestries. His fingers, surprisingly deft, danced across the keys. He hesitated for a moment, then pushed the device toward them.

"Everything," he said, "is there."

Annie leaned in, her sharp gaze fixed on the account balance glowing on the laptop screen. "That's a nice sum," Annie agreed. "Does Tania know?"

"Not about the crypto," Guru Mett admitted. "But she asked not to be made aware of the specifics. She trusts me."

"Just like Russel did?" Annie asked.

"Russel believed in Serenity Peaks. So do I." Guru Mett's voice held a warmth that belied his past deeds. "These people... this place..." His hand swept around the room before settling over his heart. "It's home."

"And the Monopoly game?" Annie asked. "What did Russel want you to do?"

"Ah, yes. The game." Guru Mett didn't flinch. "Russel knew about my past because, well, when you get close to a friend, it's hard not to share who you were before. We broke the rules here as so many do and talked about our prior lives. Things came out when we were playing board games. Not much to do around here, and Russel and I always played Monopoly. You'll understand now, why it appealed to me as the game of choice. Russel told me only that he left some kind of crime syndicate. And I told him about my vices. A few days before Russel died, he asked me to set up two private offshore accounts using his funds. I don't know how he came by this money, but he requested it be hidden in an untraceable Swiss bank account."

"Under whose name?"

Guru Mett stared at her, unsure how to deliver the news. Then, he offered, simply:

"Yours."

Annie and Ethan exchanged a glance. Guru Mett typed on his computer, pulling up the accounts in question Annie and Ethan looked at the banking information, finding a tidy sum there.

"What did he want us to do with it?" Ethan asked.

Guru Mett shrugged. "He wouldn't tell me. Said you'd know. Monopoly was the game. And now, it's your move."

Guru Mett's fingers danced across the laptop's keys. The machine hummed, processing his commands with an obedient whir. He removed a small black thumb drive from a port on the laptop, then passed it to Annie and Ethan.

"All the information is on that drive," he said, his voice a low thrum in the quiet of the yoga studio. "How to access the funds. Account numbers. Everything you need is there. Russel trusted you," Guru Mett said, his gaze shifting between them. "More than the money, more than *Serenity Peaks*... whatever he wanted you to do is his legacy."

Annie and Ethan shared a glance, the gravity of what they'd been left with suddenly hitting them both.

"One more thing," Annie said, looking at Guru Mett. "In

short order, we're going to need your help again. In fact, we're going to need the entire commune's help."

"And?"

"And I want to know if we can count on you."

"If it's for *Serenity Peaks*, you certainly can," Guru Mett confirmed.

"Good," Annie nodded.

With that, Annie and Ethan exited, leaving Guru Mett alone in his studio. He stared at the blinking cursor on his computer, finding it funny that a small world could exist within another. In one world, Guru Mett was a spiritual advisor. But in that metal trap of a computer, he was someone else entirely. Now that the two worlds had crossed, Guru Mett felt a flood of relief. He knew he needed to talk to Tania. But that could wait for another day.

CHAPTER TWENTY-EIGHT

TANIA

IN THE COMMUNE'S community garden, Tania Wildheart's hands were deep in the loam, her fingers coaxing life from the earth with an almost maternal care. She hummed a tune under her breath, notes rising and falling with the mountain breeze that swept through *Serenity Peaks*. Sunlight filtered down upon her back, warming the fabric of her vibrant blouse as she tended to the sprouts that promised a season of abundance. *Everything is going to be alright*, she thought to herself, pushing Russel's murder out of her mind.

"Tania," a voice called, shattering her illusions that everything was going to be just fine.

Tania straightened, eyes following the sound. Annie Hudson stood at the fringe of the garden, flanked by Ethan Beckett. Their appearance in Tania's tranquil oasis was unexpected and jarring. She swallowed hard.

"We need your help," Ethan said.

"Of course," Tania replied, brushing soil from her hands onto her apron. Her heart beat a sudden staccato against her ribs. "Anything."

Annie stepped forward, her gaze locked onto Tania's face

with a pleasant, inscrutable smile. "I'm close to solving it," she announced, her words light and easy. "Russel's case."

Tania felt the blood drain from her cheeks, coolness seeping into her skin despite the sun's embrace. "That's... that's great news," she managed, her voice betraying a quiver.

"I'd like to tell everyone. Together. Give the entire commune closure at the same time." Annie's eyes didn't waver, reading Tania's every flicker of emotion. "Can we arrange that?"

"Sure." Tania's nod was almost imperceptible, her mind racing with the implications of Annie's words. "Just let me know when." Tania's fingers hovered over a tender green shoot, her touch featherlight. "Actually, tonight we have a group ceremony. It's one of the more moving traditions we have. Maybe, after it's done—" she murmured, looking down at the soil on her hands.

"Perfect timing," Annie said, an edge to her voice. Then, Annie paused, realizing something. "You said the ceremony was tonight." It was a statement, not a question, but Tania answered anyway:

"Yes," Tania confirmed.

"Hmm," Annie thought aloud, chewing something over in her mind's eye. "Plan on getting the group together after the ceremony, but wait for our signal before you round them up. Ethan and I will let you know when it's time."

"Got a suspicion?" Ethan asked Annie, smiling. He knew her preference for relying on facts, but somehow— a suspicion always seemed to make its way into the mix.

Annie grinned back at him. "I do," she said. "I hope it proves to be correct. Otherwise, we may have a tricky evening on our hands."

"What evening with us *doesn't* turn out to be tricky?" Ethan answered.

"If there's nothing else, I'll just—" Tania motioned at the plants, lush and vibrant, their leaves a deep shade of green.

Different species dotted the garden, some edible, some existing purely for the joy of it all. Each was different, some with delicate flowers while others had intricate patterns on their leaves. Their roots disappeared into rich, dark, soil, feeding them what they needed to grow. Tania secretly wished she could climb under the dirt with them, but instead, she picked up her shovel and started to dig another hole.

"There's nothing else," Annie said. Tania's avoidance wasn't lost on her. In fact, she'd been expecting it. Annie turned to leave but paused, her attention caught by a barren container amidst the thriving garden beds. She approached it, her movements precise, deliberate.

"Except… That empty planter at your cabin," Annie continued. "… the one where you said you used to grow Lupine. Have you planted anymore?" Annie's question cut through the air, each word sharpened with intention.

Tania looked up at her, eyes burning, but not because of the sun. "No," Tania said, her voice shaking. Annie's question cut through the air, each word sharpened with intention.

"Of course you wouldn't," Annie said, the tone of her voice affirmative, as if she were finishing a conversation they'd never even had. "I wouldn't have replanted it, either. After what happened."

"What happened?" Tania said, her eyes watering. Pretending not to know felt almost infantile, given the way Detective Annie Hudson was looking at her.

"The Lupine. Have you ever given it to anyone?"

"Once," Tania whispered, the admission heavy, sinking deep into the soil beneath their feet.

Annie's nod was barely perceptible, a silent acknowledgment of the unsaid.

"We'll see you at the ceremony tonight," Annie offered before her and her partner turned to leave. Tania watched them depart, their steps measured, leaving her alone knee-deep in the richest soil she'd ever used.

CHAPTER TWENTY-NINE

NIGHT FELL HARD, and she didn't get back up again. Stars gleamed like pinpricks in a blanket so thick it muffled any doubts about "if" or "when"— under the darkness of a ceremonial evening, *Serenity Peaks* had become a place that felt timeless and infinite.

The residents gathered, seated on fallen logs arranged in a circle around Tania Wildheart. Her braided hair, interwoven with dried flowers, hung heavy around her face on this windless night. In the distance, crickets chirped a gentle song— one that seemed to encourage Tania with a rhythmic chant. She waited until all eyes were on her. Only then, when she was sure she had the group's full attention— did she begin.

"Ceremony," Tania began, her voice steady and clear, "is the heartbeat of our community. It reminds us that together, we are boundless." Her gaze swept over the faces before her — Fleur, with her ethereal quietude; Mark, solid as the pines that surrounded them; Guru Mett, whimsical and calm; Banks, still a mystery, his eyes unreadable behind black-rimmed glasses; Cord, pleased to be with his favorite people; and Annie and Ethan, mirroring each other like opposite halves of a coin.

"Tonight," she continued, "we affirm that conviction."

With purpose, Tania stepped aside. A path of hot coals came into view, glowing ominously in the twilight, charcoal orbs burning red like magma.

"Each step you take," Tania declared, "proves the power of our tribe."

Annie caught Banks's eye. He flinched ever so slightly. Fear. But there was no tremor in Fleur's hands, no hesitation in Mark's posture. Guru Mett sat, unperturbed. It seemed as if the other members of the commune had participated in this exercise before, and were unafraid. That left Banks, Annie, and Ethan to confront something they'd never done. Ethan squeezed Annie's shoulder—a silent pact. Banks sat alone.

"Who will hold your hand at the end of this trial?" Tania challenged, her eyes locking onto each member in turn.

Silence hung heavy, punctuated by the crackle of the coals. Someone would be waiting. Always.

"When you face these coals, focus on the people waiting for you at the end of the line. Humans were meant to live in tribes, and we can do more together than we can apart. The outside world may have forgotten that, but at *Serenity Peaks*, we promise always to catch each other. To prove this you, I volunteer as the first to cross, knowing everyone here is with me."

Tania turned, flipping her hair over her shoulder. She stepped onto the path, the coal's heat rising— a whispered challenge. Around her, the commune held its breath. Tania closed her eyes. She inhaled deeply. Over her shoulder, the group cheered.

"Step, step, step—" Mark began the chant, and the rest of the group joined in. Calmly, and without fear, Tania took a step onto the hot coals. Then another. And another. Each step was a testament to her belief in their shared strength. At the end of the fiery aisle, she turned, her presence an anchor for the next.

The group cheered as her feet touched solid Earth. Tania held up her arms, welcoming the next person.

Mark rose, his weather-beaten face betraying no fear. Feet bare, he faced the glowing embers. In the moment before he stepped on the coals, he thought about Russell and remembered the first time he'd done this exercise with the man he'd later grown to love. He looked over his shoulder at Fleur, who was still seated on a log. Her eyes connected with his. They were watering, and he knew— she was thinking of Russell, too. Mark offered her a gentle nod, then stepped onto the coals. He crossed them with ease, as if he were walking on a sidewalk. Upon reaching the end, his eyes met Tania's. She opened her arms to him as he fell onto solid ground, allowing her to pull him close. When they parted, she gave Mark's hand a squeeze, then moved aside to allow him to be an anchor for the next person.

Fleur stood, her lightness stark against the primal trial before her. Mark extended his arms wide, as if willing her strength. She stepped forward, her connection with the earth beneath her feet palpable even through the burning coals. The commune watched, enraptured by her serene confidence. Like a spirit bound to the land, she crossed with uncanny grace.

"Bravo, Fleur!" Cheers erupted as she reached the end, falling into Mark's embrace. Her arrival was a delicate seal on the grief that now connected them.

"Your turn, Cord," Tania called.

Cord smiled, leaning over to Annie and Ethan. "I love this part," he said. He leaped up and crossed the coals in a fluid, easy line, hugging Fleur when he reached the end. He turned, arms open, shouting toward the logs:

"Get in here, Mett."

Guru Mett approached, his long sweater brushing the ground. No theatrics, just quiet certainty. His beard, streaked with grey wisdom, barely quivered as he moved across the coals, each step deliberate. A collective sigh released when he joined the group, their numbers growing— a testament to the collective will.

"Annie, Ethan," Tania's voice cut through the mounting anticipation. "Your choice."

Annie exchanged a glance with Ethan. His nod was imperceptible but clear.

"We can skip this," Ethan murmured, the offer hanging between them.

"No," Annie's voice was soft, cutting through hesitation. "We've done worse," she winked at him. She peeled away from Ethan's side, her dark hair a sharp contrast to the night sky. Annie was done running from the things that caused her pain, and she hoped— somehow— walking across the coals would heal something.

She left her shoes at the start of the trail, then stepped onto the coals. She moved quickly, focused on the end of the line. Resolve powered her across the coals, every muscle tensed against the heat that tried to claim her.

She emerged on the other side, victorious, the group embracing her, making space for her stand at the trail's end as a beacon for the next to arrive— Ethan.

"Come on," she breathed, the words barely above a whisper but carrying the weight of all they had endured together. "You can do it, Ethan."

Ethan squared his shoulders, heat radiating against his skin. Eyes locked on Annie, the path of coals stretched before him—a fiery challenge. He stepped forward, each stride a testament to the trust he placed in her presence. The fire nipped at his resolve, yet he moved with unwavering focus.

He stumbled in the middle of the path, heat slipping between the coals and onto this foot. "Annie!" His voice was steady, betraying none of the trepidation that had gripped him moments ago.

"Faster!" She called, and Ethan picked up the pace, skimming the top of the burning aisle.

When he finally reached the trail's end, Ethan clasped Annie in a fierce hug, the scent of smoke clinging to them both. "I knew you could," Annie smiled at him.

"I wouldn't have," Ethan admitted, chest heaving slightly from the adrenaline. "Not without you here."

Annie's eyes met his, a silent acknowledgment of their shared strength. It wasn't just the coals they were facing—it was the haunting specter of her brother's unsolved murder, an ember that refused to die. Together, they were more than they were apart; this moment was proof.

"Alright, Banks. Your turn," Tania announced, her tone a mix of encouragement and command.

Banks hesitated, his glasses reflecting the flickering light as if revealing the tumult within. "No." His refusal cut through the night air, stark and unexpected. "I won't walk through fire for theatrics."

"Think, Banks," Tania called out, her voice laced with an edge of challenge. "Consider the fires you've endured, the trials that scorched your past."

I was alone then and I'm alone now, Banks thought to himself. He shouted, his voice pained in the night: "You people need me to prove something to you? No thanks, I'm good."

"It's not about proving anything," Tania answered quietly. "If you choose to forgo the coals tonight, we'll be here for you just the same. But you *can* conquer them. Here, you're not alone."

Banks' jaw tightened. "Stupid," he muttered, but he took his shoes off and headed to the start of the trail. "This whole thing is just—"

He stepped onto the glowing pathway. His foot hovered, then met the heat. A collective breath held as he moved, one slow, deliberate step after another. The coals crackled under his weight, a soft symphony of ember and skin.

Annie's gaze didn't waver; she dissected every microexpression, each subtle shift of Banks' muscles. There was more to this than fear—secrets lay beneath that stoic veneer. Banks struck her as someone who wasn't afraid of much, and she suspected it wasn't the fire of the coals that threatened him. Rather, it was something deeper about the nature of life in *Serenity Peaks*. It was the closeness to other people the place offered, and what that meant for someone used to being alone.

Finally, Banks reached the trail's end. The moment stretched, silence enveloping them before it shattered with applause. Tania stepped forward, arms wide. The embrace was tight, everyone joining. Except Annie, her eyes locked on Banks.

He turned to her, and their gazes collided. A flicker of something passed over his features—guilt? It vanished as quickly as it appeared, but Annie caught it and filed it away.

Tania put a hand on Banks' cheek, while Fleur and Mark patted his back. "You did," Tania said to him. "Out of many, one," Tania declared, her voice resonating in the crisp mountain air. "And now… let's celebrate!"

She motioned to a cooler filled with snacks, and a nearby thermos of hot chocolate with cups sitting beside it. The group poured themselves drinks, steam rising like the embers spiraling skyward. Laughter, chatter, and the warmth of shared victory against the night filled the wilderness. Annie took a cup— felt its heat seep into her fingers. She eyed Banks, who stood slightly apart, nursing his drink, watching the fire die.

"Quite a night, huh?" Ethan murmured beside her.

"And it's only just beginning," Annie answered. Her reply was cryptic, eyes never leaving Banks' slouched figure by the fading light.

The ceremony had ended, but the investigation—Annie's silent hunt for truth—had just found the last missing piece.

CHAPTER THIRTY

BANKS

BANKS STORMED through the wooden front door of his cabin, the echoes of the ceremony still haunting him. He thrust the door shut with a violent slam, his hand trembling. Alone now, he stumbled to the bed, the unadorned room spinning slightly as he fell onto the scratchy blanket. His chest heaved—a silent fight within. Eyes that rarely misted now stung with unwelcome moisture. Damn it.

The ceremony had touched something within Banks. A need he tried to ignore. Now, he had to collect himself.

A deep breath. Another. Banks clenched his jaw, willing away the significance of what had passed outside under the towering pines. He hated this—hated that the communal chants and earnest faces had managed to perforate his armor. But in *Serenity Peaks*, everything was designed to infiltrate, to connect. Even with someone like him.

Enough.

With mechanical movements, Banks reached for his duffel bag, and dumped carelessly on the floorboards. His fingers found the hidden seam and delved inside, extracting a sleek cell phone from its fabric womb. The screen blinked alive at his touch, illuminating the sparse furnishings with a cold glow. He'd been trying to ignore the phone— and what the person on the other end had asked him to do— for days. But now, he looked at the latest message.

UNKNOWN

Task executed?

The words hung there, stark against the backdrop of unread notifications. Banks' thumb hovered, hesitating.

UNKNOWN

Task executed?

The message pulsed with a rhythm that matched the thudding in his temples. It demanded an answer, a confirmation of duty fulfilled. And yet, Banks knew the weight behind those two words meant giving up what he had found, here. They held a command, a test, a life balanced precariously on the edge of a decision that would change everything once it was made.

UNKNOWN

Task executed?

He reread the message as if it might morph into something else. It didn't. The room felt colder, the walls inching closer. Banks closed his eyes for a moment, grappling with the gravity of his next move. This wasn't just about completing an assignment. This was about allegiance, about proving himself.

UNKNOWN

Task executed?

Banks scrolled up, looking at the previous message. A thumb swipe revealed two pictures: Annie, and Ethan. A glimpse of Annie's dark, deliberate eyes. Ethan, ever vigilant beside her. Banks' breath hitched.

UNKNOWN

Eliminate.

The directive he'd so far failed to fulfill was a grim anchor in a sea of other requests.

"Damn it," he hissed, the phone slipping from his fingers. It clattered onto the table. Banks stood, running his hands through his hair. He needed to get angry. Anger was what had led him throughout life— it always helped him do what needed to be done. He let the rage build within him, then reached for a lamp on the bedside table, tossing it to the ground. Its base broke into pieces, shards of its former self strewn across the wooden floor. Banks' pulse quickened; the anger didn't feel as good as it used to, but at least it was something.

"Focus," Banks growled to himself. He needed the anger, the fury that would shield him from the tendrils of doubt. He envisioned the faces in the photo as targets, not people, stripping them of their humanity.

"Targets," he muttered, the word a mantra to harden his resolve. The room seemed to shrink, the walls pressing in with the weight of the task at hand. Banks clenched his jaw, the image of Annie and Ethan burning behind his eyelids, goading him into the darkness he'd need to navigate tonight.

He was ready to do what needed to be done.

Deliberate, Banks began to pack. He eliminated all traces that he'd ever been here. He swept his belongings into his suitcase—a cascade of fabric and necessity—each item a testament to the transient nature of his stay in *Serenity Peaks*. Clothes, toiletries, mementos; none held significance now. Every garment hurled into the bag was another step away from this place of false tranquility. When it was done, he wiped down counters and cabinets to avoid leaving fingerprints behind.

He left a single black hoodie draped over a chair— an

outlier in the commotion. He snatched it, the fabric chilling his fingertips, a stark contrast to the warmth it promised. Slipping it over his head, he felt the shield of anonymity it offered. A dark silhouette against the backdrop of rustic idealism.

The desk drawer gave a soft creak as Banks opened it, revealing a gun and ammo he'd tucked away. Metal kissed metal as Banks loaded the gun, a quiet clink as bullets aligned with chambers. He snapped the magazine into place, the sound final, decisive. His thumb caressed the cold steel. A familiar friend.

A deep breath filled his lungs, its release a silent signal to move. He'd come back for the bags when the job was done and head far away from this place, back to the life he knew. The door closed behind him with a muted click, surrendering him to the night's embrace. Shadows clung to his form as he strode towards whatever end awaited. Duty, cloaked in darkness, propelled him forward. Whatever *Serenity Peaks* had tried to offer him, it wasn't enough. His mission, clear and unforgiving, owned him now.

CHAPTER THIRTY-ONE

AS BANKS STEPPED onto the porch of Annie and Ethan's cabin, it occurred to him that the building was an exact copy of his own lodgings. Here in *Serenity Peaks,* the cabins were built to spec. Each dwelling was similar in size, and shape — no resident was offered a cabin larger than anyone else's. That was the thing about this place— it reminded a man that he was the same as anyone else. There was no place for power, or greed. People lived the same, and they died the same.

And tonight… it was Annie and Ethan's turn to die.

Banks' fingers danced with practiced grace at the front door to the cabin, the lock yielding to his deft touch. The door whispered open. Inside, the cabin was dark. Silent. As Banks stepped forward, he imagined himself as he must look to his prey. A silhouette— a specter against the night— paused on the threshold. He slipped inside, the weight of the gun in his sweatshirt pocket a familiar comfort.

Step by cautious step, he advanced into the void, every sense straining for the telltale creak of floorboards, or the faintest rustle betraying presence. But silence clung to the evening air like cobwebs— until it didn't.

Lights blazed to life. Banks froze, hand inching towards the weapon's outline.

"Welcome," came Annie's steady voice. Banks could heat the smile in her greeting.

Eyes adjusting, Banks took in the scene. A circle of faces stared back at him. Ethan's jaw set firm; Fleur's gaze flitted, bird-like; Tania, her hands clasping and unclasping; Guru Mett, an unreadable sphinx; Cord's smirk, hiding nerves; Mark, impassive as stone. They were seated in a circle. The entire commune had gathered, minus one.

In the center, an empty chair beckoned.

"Have a seat," Annie continued, motioning with a tilt of her head at the empty chair. Beside her, Ethan stirred, drawing Bank's attention to a gun resting on his knee, pointing directly at Banks. Annie seemed to notice that the presence of the gun had registered with Banks. "An insurance policy," she said, smiling at him again. "I would've rather gone without the presence of a weapon, but Ethan here insisted—"

"It's important we're on an even playing field, don't you think?" Ethan nodded at Banks, his finger close enough to the trigger to change everything in an instant.

"You knew I'd come?" Banks asked, moving his hand toward his sweatshirt pocket.

"Before you decide to use that," she nodded at his pocket, "you really should take a seat. The game Russel left for us all to play has been quite the adventure, and I'd hate for you to miss the final round."

Banks measured the distance between them, calculated odds. Seven to one. His trained hands could make quick work of them all if he wanted to, but curiosity clawed at him. *What game?*

"Banks," Fleur said, looking up at him through her large, kitten-like eyes. "It would really mean a lot if you'd sit."

Banks felt his stomach churn and yielded as his legs carried him over to claim the empty chair.

"Fine," he grunted, the commune's collective breath a silent pressure against his back. His hand moved away from the hidden gun in his pocket. For now. "Talk."

Banks waited, his posture rigid, every muscle a coiled spring. The commune's eyes fixed on him. No one dared look away.

"I'm so pleased to have everyone here together," Annie said, clapping her hands as if she were the leader of a ragtag summer camp. "This has been a very— personal investigation — and I know how much Russel meant to you all. Tonight, I wanted everyone to come together so I could share my conclusion in this matter." Annie paused, clearing her throat. "Let's begin with a foundational element, something we all must know in order for the rest of the clues in this puzzle to fall into place. Unfortunately, Tania," Annie turned to Tania, shrugging at her. "It involves sharing details about multiple residents' pasts."

Tania bristled, looking worried at the impending breaking of commune rules. "Actually, Annie, I'd really prefer if you didn't—"

"Thank you for your understanding!" Annie exclaimed, nodding eagerly as she continued despite Tania's protests. "Before Russel Grey arrived in *Serenity Peaks*, he was a part of a criminal organization called… 'The Collective.'"

Murmurs echoed around the room. Guru Mett and Tania shared a glance. Cord's mouth dropped open, his expression dumbfounded. Only Fleur and Banks looked unmoved by this information. Fleur nodded, her blue-green eyes locked onto Banks, her expression a mix of resolve and sorrow.

"The Collective is an organized crime ring that engaged in all manner of bad behavior, from human and drug trafficking to cybercrime. They tend to find their members when they're at their most vulnerable, adopting them for life."

Annie looked at Banks as she described the group, and he resisted the urge to look away.

"Russel joined when he was young and easy to manipulate— to mold. But as the years went by, he began to have his doubts. He couldn't abide by their ways any longer," Annie continued. "And when he learned he had a teenage daughter who he'd never known— who'd been born into the Collective — he left, and he took her with him. They both sought refuge here, at *Serenity Peaks*."

There was a long moment as the realization dawned on the group. Tania gasped, putting a hand over her mouth. "Fleur, Russel was —?"

"My father," Fleur confirmed, nodding. "He thought it'd be safer for everyone if we kept it a secret."

"Because The Collective's arms reach wide," Annie nodded. "He worried they could find you, even off the grid. In that way, I supposed Russel found security but not peace," Annie thought aloud. "He realized— just as I would have— that the only way to ever ensure safety for his child was to destroy the group once and for all. He needed to dismantle what he escaped from. Otherwise, there would always be another shadow from which to run. And so, Russel's goal changed. He didn't just want to escape The Collective. He wanted the group destroyed— forever. And so, he worked on his plan. And it started..." Annie smiled at Ethan. "With us."

"With *you?*" Tania asked, confused. "But Russel was already dead when you arrived."

"True," Annie agreed. "But Russel knew about Ethan and me before either one of us learned about him, or even the Collective. Russel went through the Collective's history, seeking others who might have a similar vengeance against the group. Perhaps he realized taking them down alone was an impossibility. Maybe he understood the power of working with a group. I'd like to think he learned that here," Annie smiled at Tania. "I'd like to believe you all taught him that."

Tania's face flushed and a choking sound escaped her throat. She tried to hold back the tears, but they came anyway.

"That's why— one year ago— Russel tasked his dear confidant, Mark, with a favor."

All eyes turned to Mark, who shifted in his chair. "He asked me to take the truck and courier a letter. A letter to Annie."

"What did it say?" Tania asked.

"The letter enlisted my help with solving a murder," Annie nodded. "I realize now Russel was bringing Ethan and me back together. He was quite the game player, as you've all shared, and he was thinking long-term. I believe that he wanted me to solve a case that reminded me of the way in which my brother died. My brother was killed, and Ethan's sister was taken by a serial killer known only as the Real Estate Ripper. With what we've learned here, I now believe Russel knew the man who hurt them. And— if our digital forensics expert is right— Russel used his own access token to track crimes as they occurred, searching for the perfect similar murder. When he found one, he had Mark make sure I was brought onto the case."

"This all sounds impossible—" Tania said, waving a hand in the air. "Russel couldn't have been tracking crimes from the commune. We don't even allow personal computers here—"

"Which is why Russel retreated to his secret hideout in the desert. Every two to three weeks he would disappear—"

"To get supplies!" Tania objected.

"To visit his base and strategize his strike back at The Collective," Annie corrected her. "Russel's safe haven was a private, enclosed facility accessed by keycard. A keycard that I was just given… by Cord." Annie smiled at Cord.

Cord shifted in his seat, the flicker of guilt passing over his youthful face. He looked at Tania, her braided hair catching the light, flowers woven between the strands.

"I take things sometimes," Cord admitted softly. He looked around the room, in shame. "I just like you all so much and I'm worried one day you'll leave, and I won't have anything to remember you by. I took the keycard from Russel—"

"— from Russel, who knew you had this proclivity," Annie nodded. "And he made sure the keycard would end up with us."

Cord turned to Tania, looking at her from underneath his long eyelashes. "I took your earrings," he said, his voice barely more than a whisper.

Tania's laughter was a surprising ripple across the tense atmosphere. "I know," she said, her tone rich with affection. "Cord, you aren't a subtle person. I think most of us are aware of your habit." Nods filled the room. Tania patted Cord's knee. "They're only earrings."

Banks watched the exchange, the gun in his pocket now a leaden weight. It struck him how easy it was for the members of the commune to forgive each other. In the world he'd come from, forgiveness didn't exist, and vengeance was swift.

Annie leaned forward, her intent clear. "Unfortunately, Russel hadn't covered his tracks as well as he'd hoped. Russel knew The Collective was onto him," she continued. "The Collective had marked Russel for assassination."

Gasps filled the room. Fleur blinked, fear crossing her face.

"Russel knew he didn't have long," Annie said, eyes narrowing. "So, he laid out a trail for me to follow. He turned it into a game."

Banks felt the edges of the story closing in, its implications tightening like a noose. He was part of this narrative, and at any moment, his role would be revealed.

"Created... a puzzle?" Cord's voice cut through the silence, breaking the spell momentarily.

"Exactly," Annie confirmed. "For me to solve. When we searched his cabin, we found that he'd assigned each one of you to a game. Again, Russel understood that a group of people can do more than one individual. So, he connected each of you to a piece of the story, without giving anyone the entire truth. Cord was assigned to the game *Sorry*, because Russel trusted that Cord's good heart would lead him to confess to the items he'd stolen, including the keycard."

"I really *was* sorry," Cord said in a whisper.

"And you did the right thing and gave us the keycard," Annie reassured him. "Which I believe will allow us to access Russel's secret secured hiding spot in the desert, from which he's been keeping tabs on The Collective. But then— there was the matter of how to share the facility's location? For this, Russel left Mark's name attached to a simple game of Hot Wheels."

"He wanted me to give them the truck," Mark told the group, shrugging. "There was a map in the dashboard, with the location. It was destroyed, but—"

"We've recreated it," Annie agreed, staring straight at Banks. "We've managed to make the map again, with Fleur's help."

Banks' breath quickened. The female detective was smart. Never had he imagined that someone could take down the Collective. For the first time, he considered that the group might not be impervious to damage. And— if anyone could make good on Russel's quest— it was the woman sitting in front of him.

"Speaking of Fleur," Annie added. "Russel used her love of art to connect her to the game of Pictionary. He knew she'd kept detailed sketches of their lives before coming to the commune and trusted her to tell us the story of their past."

"He asked me before he died," Fleur said, her voice

catching in her throat. "Made me promise when the female Detective came, I'd tell her everything when she asked."

"And then— there was the game of Monopoly," Annie continued. "Left for Guru Mett, who Russel hoped would give us the funds to finance an attack against the Collective. Of course, Guru Mett was reluctant to share this information with us, given that—"

"Given that I *may* have made some risky investments with the Commune's funds," Guru Mett confessed.

Tania's mouth dropped open in horror. "Please tell me you didn't—"

"It's all there," Mett held his hands up in the air. "Ninety percent untouched and in a money market. The other ten percent... well... I invested it in crypto. We've got ten times what we started with. I just didn't want to alarm you and give you a reason to dig into my past." Guru Mett glanced at the ground. "It's not pretty."

There was a moment of silence, and then— Tania burst out laughing. "I *know*," she said.

"You know?"

"Mett, the white-collar crime you committed was all over the news." She shook her head. "We may not allow cell phones or computers, but the diner in town has a TV. I knew exactly who you were when you joined."

"And you still— let me— in?" Mett asked, shocked. "And gave me control of our money?"

Tania shrugged. "The more I got to know you, the more I believed you'd changed. This place does that to people. Changes them. Look at you," she smiled at him. "You only chose to gamble with ten percent of our money and left ninety percent alone. I'd say that's growth."

Ethan couldn't help but arch his eyebrows at Tania's naivety. Still— she had a point. Mett might not have been fully reformed, but he was, at least, improving.

"Which brings us to the final member," Annie said,

glancing at Tania. "The leader of the group. Tania Wildheart. Russel left the game *Hungry Hippos* for Tania."

"Russel," Tania said, eyes watering. "If I'd known what he was up to—" Tania stopped talking at the thought, looking at the ground instead.

"To understand this one, what you all need to know is simply this," Annie continued. "Russel wasn't murdered. Was he Tania?"

Tania shook her head, her face flushed. "No," she said in a whisper. "No— I realize now— but it's too awful to say out loud."

Annie lifted the burden from her, and declared the truth:

"Russel Grey killed himself. He knew he was on borrowed time. And he decided to go out his own way rather than let the Collective do it for him. He planned the puzzle in advance, knowing a murder would force me to investigate. And he killed himself in the most painless way possible: by overdosing on the Lupine plant."

"Isn't that the little purple flowers?" Guru Mett asked. He turned to Tania. "The ones you grow by your door?"

"It is," Tania agreed. She looked at Fleur, deep regret in her eyes. "When he asked me for some dried Lupine, I thought it was to help him sleep. If I'd known what he had planned I never would have—"

"It's okay," Fleur said, pain crossing her face. "He would have found another way to do it if you hadn't given him the Lupine. Once he made up his mind, that was it."

Tania's fingers twisted the hem of her vibrant skirt. "He said he needed it... to rest easy. I really thought he meant sleep." Her voice broke on the word, a fissure through which her pain echoed. "I didn't know he was going to..."

"To end his own story," Annie finished for her, a solemn note in her otherwise crisp tone.

"Before *they* could," Ethan said.

"Russel was moves ahead of everyone," Annie stated,

locking eyes with each person in the circle. "He knew his fate rested in his own hands. He built the game and put himself— and all of us— on the board as pieces."

"His final act," Ethan added, "was one last stand against The Collective."

"Russel wanted his exit to be *his* choice," Annie said firmly. "Not theirs. He knew there was an assassin on the way to the Commune, coming to destroy him. And in fact, Russel was correct. That very assassin arrived just hours after Russel's death. He was too late, of course. But he'd come with a mission. And— when he arrived and realized Russel was already dead— I'm sure he was assigned a new one. Is that correct…" Annie paused, "… Banks?"

Heads swiveled around the room as everyone turned to stare at Banks. He rose slowly from his chair, his eyes still locked on the gun that sat perched on Ethan's knee.

""Russel left us a game connected to the assassin who had not yet arrived when he died. It was Connect Four. He said 'the newest one' would 'connect' for us, and now it has. Banks, would you like to tell the room how you planned to kill Russel?" Annie smiled at him as if she were inviting him to tea. "Or, perhaps you could share some stories about what it's like to be a member of the Collective? I know we're all curious!"

Banks waited a moment, his eyes scanning the people he'd come to think of as a strange sort of home. Images of his past flashed before his eyes. Of course, he could share stories about the Collective. But they were the kind of stories a man kept to himself— the bloody things a person tucked under their pillow before falling asleep at night.

"Russel proved the first thing they tell you when you join to be true," Banks said, his voice low and throaty.

"And what's that?" Annie asked.

"The first thing they teach you is that the only way out of the Collective… is death."

"*Is* that the only way, Banks?" Annie challenged, her voice even. A bit of regret marked the lines around her mouth. She had hoped Banks would take a different path— but it seemed he'd made his choice.

"Death is the only way out," Banks answered. And with that, he pulled the gun from his pocket and dove across the room, taking cover behind the dresser just as Ethan let the first bullet fly.

CHAPTER THIRTY-TWO

ETHAN'S BULLET landed with a thud in the wooden slats that lined the cabin's back wall. Banks managed to get off a shot of his own in return, but it ricochetted in the wrong direction, shattering the cabin's glass window. It wasn't like Banks to be such a bad marksman, but some small piece of him worried about hitting the innocent members of the commune. Now was not the time to be stupid. Not the time to be soft. His next bullet would find its mark— he'd make sure of that.

Banks crouched behind the dresser, his breath moving in short, sharp bursts. He heard— but didn't see— muffled protests and exclamations from the group. It sounded as if the members of the commune were trying to talk Ethan down. But Banks knew how men like him operated. He didn't blame Ethan for shooting first. He would've done the same.

Banks snuck a peek at the group, his back pressed against the rough wood of the dresser, gun gripped tight in his hand. A quick scan told him all he needed to know, from Annie's wide-eyed stare to Ethan's taut jaw, then to the stillness of the commune members. Silence thickened. Each heartbeat thundered in his ears.

"Enough," came Tania's voice, slicing through the tension.

She stepped forward, her vibrant attire stark against the room's neutral tones.

"Get back or I'll shoot," Banks shouted.

Tania ignored him. She stepped forward, glancing around the side of the dresser, her arms held high in the air. For a brief moment, her gaze locked onto Banks.

"You're shaking," she observed, not unkindly.

"Of course, he is," Ethan quipped from across the room, hands raised in mock defense. "He's got the aim of a stormtrooper."

The remark hung in the air, an absurd lifeline against the gravity of the moment. A few stifled chuckles broke free, easing the collective breath being held.

"Your weapon doesn't scare us, Banks," Tania continued, her voice steady. She took a step back for safety, but her eyes never wavered from the dresser. "Come out."

Banks tightened his hold on the gun. Yet, beneath the skepticism, something wavered. He blinked, once, twice, as if to clear his vision or perhaps his conscience. He was a good shot. He could take out Annie and Ethan, then escape this place and never return.

"You're part of this now," Tania said firmly. "*Serenity Peaks* is your home. Or it can be…"

"Not if he shoots me," Banks' voice rang out from the back of the room. "Tell him to drop the gun."

"Can't," Ethan said, stepping in front of Annie, gun still drawn. "Tania may think the best of you, but I won't gamble people's lives. You understand."

Banks' lips twitched, almost imperceptibly. His gun lowered an inch. "I do," he said from behind the dresser. "If it means anything, the only lives I've been instructed to take are yours… and *hers*," Banks said, smiling. "The rest of the commune goes free. Just need the three of us in the room alone."

"That's not happening tonight," Ethan called back at him.

"Ethan's a good shot," Annie's voice rang out. "If I were you, Banks, I'd listen to Tania."

Guru Mett rose, the folds of his robe whispering against the wooden floor. Banks could just make out his slippers stepping closer to the dresser, their wooly lining visible under a slat between the dresser's bottom and the cabin floor.

"Banks," Guru Mett said. "When a forest burns down, new life grows in its place. I know it doesn't feel like it, but you can start your life over. Right now. All you have to do is drop the gun and step out from behind that dresser. Everyone here knows what it's like to come from a different past. But you can leave that behind."

"None of you know the first thing about my life—" Banks whispered, more to himself than anyone else.

Mark, rugged and resolute, advanced with deliberate steps. "I became a terrorist to save trees. Thought I was doing right by Earth— before I realized I was doing wrong by my fellow man." He stopped, just an arm's length away from the dresser. "When I came here, nobody cared who I was before I joined. You can leave it behind."

The gun in Banks' hand felt heavier. A burden rather than a shield.

"Every soul in this room," Mark's tone intensified, "has faced their dark. We've stumbled, fallen, but together—we rise."

The gun dipped, an inch, maybe two. Banks' arm ached, the metal cold against his skin.

"See this place?" Tania's voice cut through the silence, her braided hair swaying as she stepped into the gap between them. "It's about new beginnings. It's about community. You're not alone anymore. All you have to do is trust us."

"He's not going to shoot any of us," Annie said, her voice a quiet light in the chaos. All heads turned, staring at her.

Banks' heart skipped a beat. He wondered what the Detective knew about him.

"Banks won't shoot any of us," Annie continued, "Because deep down, he wants a new beginning. We found his lantern in the forest. He'd written *The Collective* on it. You wrote that because you're ready to leave them, aren't you Banks?"

There was no answer, but Tania seemed to let Annie's words wash over her. Over the years, she had helped many people move on from terrible situations. And it always required just a little bit of risk. She stepped forward.

Banks jolted as a figure appeared beside him. It was Tania, peeking around the edge of the dresser, hands still aloft. Banks pointed the gun at her but she didn't flinch. Instead, she crouched down next to him and sat at his side, legs crossed. She leaned her head against the dresser, making no movement to try and disarm Banks. Instead, she looked at him, her eyes still. "Trust me, the way I'm trusting you."

Banks hesitated. The gun, once a cold extension of his will, now seemed a foreign object in his hand. He watched it, as if for the first time, noting the way the metal glinted dully in the low light.

"They'll never let me go," Banks whispered, something inside him breaking wide open. "The Collective will find me. None of you will be safe if I stay here and they'll never stop hunting me."

"Banks," Tania began, her voice firm yet imbued with a warmth that seemed to fill every corner of the dimly lit room, "we can keep you safe. You're not alone now."

"How?" Banks wondered.

"I've been thinking it's about time we relocated the entire commune," Tania sighed, a hint of resolve lacing her tone. "I think the cabins are getting a little worn. Don't you all agree?" She called to the group. A chorus of affirmations answered back. Tania returned her gaze to Banks. "Fleur won't be safe unless we move. And neither will you. We can all start over somewhere new— together."

Fleur emerged from the huddle of nodding commune members, her figure almost ghostlike against the stark backdrop of the wooden cabin. "My dad was brave. Brave enough to give us a fresh start. He'd want the same for you, Banks. Leaving The Collective isn't impossible. If I could do it, you can too."

The floorboards creaked under Banks' shifting weight. The moment felt defining. He knew this was a chance he'd never get again. If life had taught him anything, it was that directions were defined with a split-second choice. Left. Right. Each decision brought a man closer to or further away from who he really was.

"What do you think, Mett?" Tania called out. "Do we have enough money to move somewhere new?"

"More than enough," Guru Mett confirmed.

Tania turned back to Banks, holding out a hand. "So… what'll it be? Shoot the detectives? Or start a new life?"

Banks' fingers trembled, the gun's weight now a burden too heavy to bear. He stared at it, the cold metal no match for the warmth spreading through the room—a tangible shift from fear to something akin to hope.

"Put it down, Banks," Tania urged, her voice the steady beat of a heart unafraid.

In one smooth motion, he placed the gun in her hand, the weapon's surrender a soft, new beginning. Tania took it from him, placing it into the pocket of her skirt. Together, they stepped out from behind the dresser.

Exhales filled the space. Smiles broke.

"Good choice," Ethan muttered, lowering his own weapon, but keeping his eyes fixed on Banks in case he made another move.

Tania stepped forward, the dried flowers in her hair askew

and tussled. She looked like she'd been through a war, and she got down to business without hesitation. "Get packing, everyone. We move in the morning," she announced. Her gaze swept across the faces before her, each one etched with stories of pasts left behind. "Together."

Heads nodded, determination mirrored in their eyes.

"Cord, can you make a list of all the communal items that we'll need to pack up? Make sure we leave nothing behind?" Tania asked.

"No problem," Cord answered, his eyes wide at the idea of leaving the commune behind.

"You got an idea of where we'll go?" Mark asked.

"We'll start somewhere temporary," Tania's words were calm, collected. "Then, we'll find a new forever home."

"Protection," Banks said, almost surprised to hear his own voice participating in the group planning. "We'll need to go somewhere remote for protection. The Collective will assume we'll pick a similar mountain environment, so we should move someplace different. The desert, or something tropical."

"I'm feeling an island," Guru Mett smiled.

"We'll vanish," Tania agreed. "Become whispers on the wind."

"Whispers," Fleur echoed softly. She couldn't help but glance at Banks. She *should* hate him for what he'd done—what he'd tried to do. But she knew what he had come from better than most and understood the need for redemption.

"Start fresh," Banks murmured, meeting each gaze. "Together."

Tania turned to Annie and Ethan. "I assume the two of you will be moving on to the location Russel left for you?"

"Seems like it," Annie agreed. "But we'll never forget each and every one of you." Her eyes lingered on Banks, who had been given the chance to start again. Despite her dislike of criminals, Annie couldn't help but hope he wouldn't waste the opportunity.

The room buzzed with energy, a hive alive with purpose. Banks stood among them, no longer the outsider with a gun, but a member of a family he never expected to find.

CHAPTER THIRTY-THREE

ANNIE'S BOOTS crunched over fallen leaves as she stood outside the collection of cabins that constituted *Serenity Peaks*. The moon hung heavy in the sky, casting a silver glow over the buzzing commune.

"It'll never be the same," a voice said beside her. It was Ethan, at her arm as he always had been. He had a way of putting what Annie was feeling into words when she couldn't do it on her own. "They've lost everything."

Annie watched the members of the commune buzz about the cabins. Cord shuffled beside Guru Mett, going over a list of items. Fleur emerged from a cabin, Mark at her heels, their arms full of what looked to be her drawing and painting supplies.

"Not everything," Annie said.

Just then, Tania approached, her arms crossed. "Time for you two to hit the road, I suppose," Tania said.

Annie looked away, a strange feeling rising in her chest. "I'm no good at goodbyes."

Tania's hands rested on her hips, a silhouette framed by the chaos of departure. "Goodbye?" She let out a laugh. "This isn't an end, Annie. It's a continuation."

Annie nodded, about to reply when a metallic jingle sliced through the conversation. Mark stood a few feet away, keys to the truck spinning around his finger. He lobbed them toward Annie, who caught them mid-air with a practiced hand.

"Take them down," he said, the intensity in his eyes matching the gravity of his words.

"Down to the ground," echoed Fleur, stepping up beside him. Her hand extended, fingers unfurling to reveal a folded map, its edges worn but the lines fresh, ink still bold. She passed it to them. "Mark and I recreated it as best we could, but I have a feeling you're still going to need to do some digging to get the exact location of my Dad's safe house."

"With Annie, that should be no problem," Mark smiled.

"We'll find it," said Annie, pocketing the key and the map. Resolve hardened as her gaze met Ethan's eyes. Across the commune, a shadowed figure stepped out of a cabin, approaching them in a hunched posture: it was Banks come to make amends. He approached with caution, keeping space between himself and Ethan.

"If you need anything, I can help," Banks said, acting as if moments earlier he hadn't intended to shoot them both. He paused, seeming to catch the look in Ethan's eye. "I mean it," he offered. "I'm starting over. This is a new me."

Ethan scanned Banks from head to toe, then reached into his bag, removing a burner phone from an interior pocket and pressing it into Banks' hand. The device was cold, utilitarian.

"Yours now," Ethan said, voice low but clear. "We call, you answer."

"Understood." Banks' fingers closed around the phone, his nod slow, resolute.

"Don't try to return call the number we use— it won't work. You're an informant and that's all," Ethan continued, "Can we count on you?"

"You can," Banks affirmed, his gaze unwavering, a silent

promise lingering in the air. "I want The Collective finished as much as anyone. My life might depend on it."

Annie watched the exchange with hawk-like intensity. Then, she shifted her focus to the white pickup truck that sat parked at the ready. She spun the key around in her hands and nodded at Ethan. Together, they headed for the truck. The doors slammed shut with a quiet thud that seemed to signal an end to their time in the commune.

"Ready?" Ethan asked, already behind the wheel.

"Let's go," Annie replied, her tone even, betraying nothing of the spiraling thoughts within.

The engine roared to life, a rumble that faded into the symphony of the wilderness. Dust billowed behind them as they left *Serenity Peaks*, the commune shrinking into a speck in the review mirror. Annie held the hand-drawn map high, considering their next destination.

"Answers in the desert?" Ethan's voice cut through the hum of the road.

"Maybe," Annie said, her gaze fixed on the horizon, where the stars twinkled overhead.

"Think Banks has really turned a corner?" Ethan probed further, stealing a glance at Annie.

Annie paused, thinking about what it meant to be part of a group. Banks had the opportunity to start again, this time— with a team behind him. Through their travels, Annie and Ethan had met so many people worth fighting for. And— even though a barren desert awaited them— Annie knew for sure they weren't alone anymore.

"I'm counting on it," she replied, her voice steady, a mirror of Banks' earlier assurance. Conviction fueled her words, a tether to the hope that all people deserved second chances.

Annie took in the expanse of horizon that revealed itself over the edge of the mountains. She knew— somewhere out there— The Collective was waiting for them. Looking for them.

And Annie couldn't wait to be found.

———

To continue the adventure, read "Murder in the Desert," Book Five in the Private Investigator Annie Hudson Mystery Series. Available now!

MORE FROM VALERIE BRANDY

THE ANNIE HUDSON REAL ESTATE MYSTERY SERIES:

- "Murder Behind the Gates" — The Private Investigator Annie Hudson Mystery Series, Book One.
- "Murder in the Penthouse" — The Private Investigator Annie Hudson Mystery Series, Book Two.
- "Murder on the Commune" — The Private Investigator Annie Hudson Mystery Series, Book Four.
- "Murder in the Desert" — The Private Investigator Annie Hudson Mystery Series, Book Five. Coming Soon.

THE PREDATOR / PREY THRILLER SERIES:

- "Trail of Obsession" — The Predator / Prey Thriller Series, Book One.
- "Lies Run Deep" — The Predator / Prey Thriller Series, Book Two.
- "The Trap is Set" — The Predator / Prey Thriller Series, Book Three.
- "The Woman in the Wind" — The Predator / Prey Thriller Series, Book Four.

COMING SOON:

THE REBECCA ORANGE COZY CASTLE MYSTERY SERIES

- Mystery at Monrovia Castle — Book One
- A Victim in the Village — Book Two
- A Royal Ruse — Book Three

Most books available in large print!

LETTER FROM THE AUTHOR

Dear Reader,

Thank you for dedicating your time to the world of Annie Hudson and the Real Estate Mystery series! I'm a screenwriter and filmmaker coming to books from Film & TV, but one thing I love about books in particular, is connecting directly with a community of readers. It's very special to be able to speak with you and hear what you want from characters in our novels.

I hope you'll reach out to me by joining my mailing list at the link below! I love to keep my readers updated on new releases, offer advanced copies, free giveaways of novellas, sneak previews, and more.

If you liked Annie Hudson, I hope you'll keep reading the rest of the series, which continues to grow!

And if you want to read more from me in general, I hope you'll check out the list of my books on the previous page.

Warmly,

— *Valerie Brandy*

www.valeriebrandy.com